PUNCH OUT

Fists smashed into Fargo, sending heavy jolts through his body. But he stayed upright and fought back. He had dropped his gun when the first man tackled him, but he still had his fists.

He slammed a punch into the middle of a man's face, then bent to the side and snapped a kick into another man's midsection. That bought him a little room, but the respite lasted only a split second, just long enough for Fargo to drag in a breath. Then one of the other men landed on his back and looped an arm around his throat. . . .

THE
TRAILSMAN

#313

TEXAS
TIMBER WAR

by

Jon Sharpe

A SIGNET BOOK

SIGNET
Published by New American Library, a division of
Penguin Group (USA) Inc., 375 Hudson Street,
New York, New York 10014, USA
Penguin Group (Canada), 90 Eglinton Avenue East, Suite 700, Toronto,
Ontario M4P 2Y3, Canada (a division of Pearson Penguin Canada Inc.)
Penguin Books Ltd., 80 Strand, London WC2R 0RL, England
Penguin Ireland, 25 St. Stephen's Green, Dublin 2,
Ireland (a division of Penguin Books Ltd.)
Penguin Group (Australia), 250 Camberwell Road, Camberwell, Victoria 3124,
Australia (a division of Pearson Australia Group Pty. Ltd.)
Penguin Books India Pvt. Ltd., 11 Community Centre, Panchsheel Park,
New Delhi - 110 017, India
Penguin Group (NZ), 67 Apollo Drive, Rosedale, North Shore 0632,
New Zealand (a division of Pearson New Zealand Ltd.)
Penguin Books (South Africa) (Pty.) Ltd., 24 Sturdee Avenue,
Rosebank, Johannesburg 2196, South Africa

Penguin Books Ltd., Registered Offices:
80 Strand, London WC2R 0RL, England

First published by Signet, an imprint of New American Library,
a division of Penguin Group (USA) Inc.

First Printing, November 2007
10 9 8 7 6 5 4 3 2 1

The first chapter of this book previously appeared in *Shanghaied Six-Guns*,
the three hundred twelfth volume in this series.

Copyright © Penguin Group (USA) Inc., 2007
All rights reserved

 REGISTERED TRADEMARK—MARCA REGISTRADA

Printed in the United States of America

PUBLISHER'S NOTE
This is a work of fiction. Names, characters, places, and incidents either are
the product of the author's imagination or are used fictitiously, and any resemblance to actual persons, living or dead, events, or locales is entirely
coincidental.

The publisher does not have any control over and does not assume any
responsibility for author or third-party Web sites or their content.

The Trailsman

Beginnings . . . they bend the tree and they mark the man. Skye Fargo was born when he was eighteen. Terror was his midwife, vengeance his first cry. Killing spawned Skye Fargo, ruthless, cold-blooded murder. Out of the acrid smoke of gunpowder still hanging in the air, he rose, cried out a promise never forgotten.

The Trailsman they began to call him all across the West: searcher, scout, hunter, the man who could see where others only looked, his skills for hire but not his soul, the man who lived each day to the fullest, yet trailed each tomorrow. Skye Fargo, the Trailsman, the seeker who could take the wildness of a land and the wanting of a woman and make them his own.

The piney woods of East Texas, 1860—where danger for the Trailsman lurks in the forest thickets.

1

The big man in buckskins raced his horse along the bank of the bayou. The area was thickly wooded, so the magnificent Ovaro stallion had to weave around and through clumps of loblolly pines and cypress trees. Even though the sun was shining overhead, the forest canopy ensured that this part of eastern Texas remained in perpetual shadow.

Skye Fargo's lake blue eyes narrowed as he heard the rattle of more gunshots. The shooting had started a couple of minutes earlier as he made his way through the area, and the swift urgency of the reports told Fargo that trouble had erupted somewhere in front of him.

Some parts of this forest were all but impenetrable, and as Fargo reined his black-and-white mount to a halt and listened to the gunfire, he had considered staying out of it for a change. Whatever was going on, he might not be able to reach the spot in time to help anyone.

But that thought had been fleeting. Fargo wasn't the sort of man to ignore someone else's danger. Moving as fast as possible, he had headed in the direction of the shots.

By the time he reached the bayou, though, the gunfire had shifted. The shots now came from somewhere upstream. Fargo turned the Ovaro to follow them.

As he rode, he became aware of another sound—a deep, throaty *chug-chug-chug* that he recognized as the noise of a steam engine. He reined the Ovaro around a bend and came in sight of a stern-wheeled riverboat churning through the waters of the bayou.

Men in canoes paddled after the riverboat, and other men who ran along the banks peppered the vessel with rifle fire. A few puffs of powder smoke from the riverboat told Fargo that someone on board was trying to put up a fight, but they weren't mustering much of one.

The attackers had to be river pirates, Fargo thought. No one else would have any reason to try to stop the boat by force like that.

Fargo reached for the Henry rifle that jutted from a sheath strapped to the Ovaro's saddle. He cranked the repeater's loading lever as he brought the rifle to his shoulder. Three canoes pursued the riverboat, and Fargo aimed at the waterline of the one closest to the vessel. He sent a couple of bullets smashing through the canoe's hull just below the surface of the bayou, then shifted his aim to the second canoe.

The men in the first canoe barely had time to realize what had happened before Fargo drilled the second canoe as well. Both of the little craft began taking on water. With yells of alarm, the pirates abandoned their pursuit of the riverboat and turned to wave their arms and point at Fargo. The men paddling the third canoe dropped their paddles and picked up rifles. They started firing at the big man on the black-and-white horse.

So did the men on the banks of the bayou. As the riverboat chugged on around another bend, the pirates turned their attention to the man who had interrupted their attack on it. Shots blasted out, further shattering what had been the peaceful stillness of the piney woods, and Fargo heard bullets ripping through the air around his head.

2

He had shot holes in the canoes, instead of in the men paddling them, because he didn't know all the details of what was going on and didn't want to kill somebody needlessly. Also, shooting somebody who wasn't even aware of his presence went against the grain for Fargo.

But now they were trying to kill him, so all restraints were off. Fargo's Henry cracked swiftly and mercilessly. One of the men in the third canoe toppled out of the little craft, landing in the bayou with a great splash of murky water. A man on the near bank fell as well, also ventilated by a slug from Fargo's rifle. A third man clutched a bullet-shattered shoulder and howled in pain.

Even though the pirates outnumbered Fargo by more than twelve to one, his deadly accurate fire must have unnerved them. The men on the far bank bolted for cover, disappearing into the trees. So did the ones on the nearer bank. And the men in the canoes paddled hard for the opposite shore, giving up the fight.

The two canoes Fargo had holed sank before they got there, with the men inside them floundering into the water and swimming for the bank. The frantic desperation of their thrashing reminded Fargo that alligators lurked in many of these East Texas streams.

Fargo held his fire and let the men flee. The canoe that was still afloat reached the shore, and the men inside it leaped out and dragged the craft onto the bank. The swimmers clambered out of the bayou and joined them. They all vanished quickly, because they had to take only a few steps before the thicket swallowed them up.

Fargo reined the Ovaro away from the bank and moved back into the woods himself, not wanting to leave himself exposed to any bushwhackers' bullets. He brought the stallion to a halt and sat there listening, an intent expression on his ruggedly handsome face with its close-cropped dark beard. The forest was quiet. All the shooting had spooked the birds and small animals and made them fall silent.

When Fargo was satisfied that the pirates had fled, rather than doubling back to try to jump him, he slid the Henry in the saddle sheath and hitched the Ovaro into motion again.

A few minutes later he hit the trail he had been following earlier, before leaving it to seek out the source of the gunfire. The trail ran west out of Louisiana toward the settlement of Jefferson, roughly paralleling Big Cypress Bayou. But since the trail twisted and turned due to the varying thickness of the forest, and the bayou followed an equally meandering path, sometimes they were within sight of each other and sometimes they weren't.

As the broad, slow-moving stream came into view again, Fargo was surprised to see that the riverboat had pulled in close to the bank and come to a halt. It had to be bound for Jefferson, which was still several miles away, Fargo reckoned. The big paddle wheel at the rear of the boat had stopped turning, but smoke rose from the twin stacks, showing that the engine still had steam up.

Fargo cut across a field dotted with pine and cypress to reach the bayou. His keen eyes scanned the decks and didn't see anyone moving around. Crates were stacked on the main deck—goods bound for Jefferson, no doubt.

The steamboats that plied these waters came up the Mississippi River from New Orleans and veered off into the Red River north of Baton Rouge, then followed the Red to Shreveport, Louisiana. From Shreveport the boats steamed up Big Cypress Bayou to sprawling Caddo Lake, which straddled the border between Louisiana and Texas and, according to local legend, had been formed by the tremendous earthquake that had shaken the whole middle part of the country nearly fifty years earlier.

Beyond Caddo Lake, Big Cypress Bayou continued to flow westward and took the paddle wheelers all the way to Jefferson. That was as far into Texas as the river traffic could penetrate, but it was far enough to open up all of eastern Texas to the rest of the world.

As a result, Jefferson wasn't the backwoods settlement it might have been otherwise, but rather a sophisticated, fast-growing city that rivaled Galveston in importance as Texas's second-largest port.

The flow of commerce wasn't all one way, either. Numerous cotton plantations were located in the area, and in the past decade, logging operations had moved in as well to harvest the riches of the hardwood forests. On the return trips, the riverboats that came to Jefferson were loaded with bales of cotton and stacks of timber. At first the loggers had tried floating the felled trees down the bayou, but the current was so slow that it proved to be impractical. Riverboats had turned out to be the answer.

Fargo was well aware of all this, his fiddle-footed ways having taken him through the region several times in the past. He knew this riverboat wouldn't have stopped along here unless something else was wrong, so he swung down from the saddle and looped the reins around the horn. The Ovaro was well trained and would stay put.

"Hello the boat!" Fargo called in his deep, powerful voice. "Permission to come aboard?"

He gathered his muscles to make the leap from the bank to the deck. Instead he jumped backward as a shot rang out and a bullet smacked into the bank ahead of him.

"Permission denied!" a man's voice bellowed.

The voice and the shot both came from the thicket of crates on the main deck. Fargo's hand dropped instinctively to the butt of the big Colt revolver holstered on his right hip, but he left the gun where it was since he couldn't see anybody to shoot at. Anyway, he figured that had been a warning shot, rather than one intended to hit him.

"Hold your fire, damn it!" he said. "I don't mean you any harm." A grim smile tugged at his mouth. "Fact of the matter is, I'm the hombre who chased off those pirates who were trying to board you, back down the bayou."

A man emerged from behind the pile of cargo, carrying a rifle. "That so?" he asked. The thick wooden peg that replaced his left leg from the knee down made a clumping sound on the deck as he moved. He was tall and scrawny, with a gray spade beard and a battered old river-man's cap crammed down on a bald head. He went on. "What the hell business was it of yours, anyway?"

"It looked to me like you folks were in trouble, so I decided to help," Fargo replied. "Simple as that. Just like I figure something else is wrong now, or you wouldn't have stopped here. You'd have gone on and made port in Jefferson."

"Got it all figured out, ain't you?" The man spat into the bayou but kept the rifle trained on Fargo. "What's your name, mister?"

"Skye Fargo."

The gaunt old-timer's eyes widened in recognition. "I heard of you," he said. "You're the fella they call the Trailsman."

"Sometimes," Fargo admitted.

"And you ain't an outlaw nor a pirate, leastways not that I recollect." Finally, the man lowered the rifle he held in his gnarled but strong-looking hands. "All right, come aboard, if you're of a mind to."

Fargo's powerfully muscled form made the jump from the bank to the deck of the riverboat without any trouble.

"I'm Caleb Thorn, the engineer o' this boat," the old-timer went on. "We're obliged to you for your help, mister. If you hadn't come along when you did, that dad-blasted bunch o' river rats might've boarded us."

"Where is everybody?" Fargo asked. "You can't be the only one on board."

"The passengers, what few there are of 'em, are in their cabins. They all run for cover when the shootin' started, and I don't blame 'em. There ain't no crew 'cept for me and a couple o' firemen, and one o' them got shot during the ruckus. The other boy's tendin' to him now. And the cap'n's up in the wheelhouse, along with—"

Thorn was interrupted by a voice that called down from the tall wheelhouse perched on top of the riverboat's two decks. "Caleb! Whoever that is, if he knows anything about doctoring, send him up here! I think the captain's about to bleed to death!"

The voice belonged to a woman, and as Fargo looked up at the wheelhouse, he saw the sunlight that penetrated along the bayou shining on blond hair. He caught just a glimpse of her face as she leaned out one of the wheelhouse windows for a moment before ducking back inside, but that was enough to tell him that she was lovely.

"Damn it!" Thorn burst out. "Cap'n Russell was hit by one of them bastards durin' the shootin'. Can you give the gal a hand, Fargo?"

"I'm already on my way," Fargo said as he strode toward one of the steep sets of stairs that led to the upper deck and the wheelhouse.

It took him only a moment to reach the wheelhouse. When he opened the door and stepped inside, he saw crimson splashed across the chart table. On the other side of the room, which had windows all around for an unimpeded view of the bayou, a man sat on a three-legged stool and leaned against a cabinet. His face was pale and drawn, and his eyes were closed as if he had passed out. The left sleeve of his shirt was soaked with blood.

The young woman who leaned over him, holding an equally blood-soaked cloth to his upper arm, turned a frantic gaze toward Fargo and said, "I can't stop the bleeding."

Fargo didn't have time to appreciate her beauty. He stepped past her, reached to the wounded man's midsection, and unbuckled the belt that was cinched around his waist. Fargo pulled the belt free, wrapped it around the man's arm above the injury, and twisted it as tight as he could. The blood welling out of the bullet hole in the captain's arm slowed to a trickle.

"I'll hold this," Fargo told the young woman. "Get me some sort of rod, about the thickness of a gun barrel."

"Where would I—" the woman began.

The wounded man opened his eyes, demonstrating that he wasn't unconscious after all. "There are some . . . spare wheel spokes . . . ," he rasped, "over there in . . . that cabinet."

He pointed with his right hand, which trembled quite a bit. The woman looked where he was indicating and came back with a wooden spoke that she handed to Fargo.

He thrust it into a loop he had made with the belt and turned it, tightening the makeshift tourniquet even more. "Now I need some strips of cloth to tie this in place," he said. "Your petticoat will do."

She flushed but pulled up the long skirt of her dark blue dress. She tore several strips from the bottom of her petticoat and, following Fargo's directions, tied them around the captain's arm so that the spoke couldn't move and release the pressure on the belt.

The bleeding from the wound had almost stopped, and the man's eyes were closed again. This time he seemed to actually be unconscious.

Fargo said to the woman, "You can't leave that tourniquet on there for very long, but it ought to be all right until you can get to Jefferson. There'll be a doctor there who can patch him up."

"That's all well and good," she said, "but we may not be able to get to Jefferson. Captain Russell's pilot quit in Shreveport, so he's been navigating by himself. He's the only one who knows where all sandbars and snags are. He has to handle the wheel."

"He's in no shape to do that," Fargo muttered. "But a boat with such a shallow draft as this one doesn't need much water to get through. I'll take the wheel."

The woman stared at him. "Are you sure you know what you're doing?"

Fargo smiled and said, "You can take over if you want."

"No, that's all right," she said with a quick shake of her head. "I've been on a lot of riverboats, but I never piloted one."

"I have," Fargo said, "but it's been a while."

In truth, his wandering life had been so eventful, as he crossed the frontier from the Mississippi to the Pacific and the Rio Grande to the Yukon, that there weren't very many things he *hadn't* tried his hand at, at one time or another.

He leaned out the open wheelhouse window and called, "Thorn!"

The old-timer appeared two decks below, on the boat's bow. He cupped his hands around his mouth and shouted, "How's the cap'n?"

"I think he'll live," Fargo replied. "Give us some steam!"

Even from up in the wheelhouse, he could see Caleb Thorn's eyes widen in surprise. "You're assumin' command?" the engineer asked.

"That's right."

"Well, then, aye, aye, Cap'n Fargo!"

Fargo grunted. He had been called a lot of things

in his life, but as far as he could recall, Captain Fargo hadn't been one of them until now.

But there was a first time for everything, even for the Trailsman.

2

Fargo whistled to the stallion, then moved to take the wheel. He spotted a rubber speaking tube hanging from the wheelhouse ceiling. He grabbed it, blew into it, and yelled, "Reverse one-quarter!"

The rumble of the engines grew louder, and the big paddle wheel at the stern began to turn, making slow revolutions in the opposite of its usual direction. As the paddles bit into the water of the bayou, the boat moved away from the bank. Fargo turned the wheel, adjusting the rudder so that as the boat backed up, it straightened its course as well.

"Ahead one-half!" Fargo called into the tube.

The paddle wheel slowed to a stop. Water sluiced off the paddles. Then it began to revolve in the other direction, forcing the vessel upstream against the sluggish current. The three boilers and the twin engines they powered were more than enough to overcome the current.

"Well, we're moving," the young woman said. "I just hope you know what you're doing."

Fargo smiled at her. "You and me both, miss."

He had to keep his attention on the bayou in front of him, but in the brief glance he had just taken at her, he had noted that her eyes were a beautiful shade of blue. Her fair hair was thick and piled on top of her head in an elaborate arrangement of curls. The dress she wore was elegant rather than flashy, but its square-cut neckline was low enough to reveal the upper third or so of her breasts. The creamy, smooth-skinned swells were as lovely as the rest of her.

"What's your name?" Fargo asked.

"Shouldn't you be concentrating on piloting this boat?"

"Don't worry. I'm paying attention to where I'm going," Fargo assured her. He glanced over at the bank and saw the Ovaro moving along it, keeping pace with the riverboat.

Fargo went on. "Ideally, we'd have a pilot who knows these waters here in the wheelhouse, and a boy up on the bow with a line and a plumb bob, marking the fathoms and calling them up to us. But we'll manage. It's not far to Jefferson."

"Captain Russell managed to get the boat to shore before he passed out. I didn't realize he was wounded so badly until I saw all the blood." A shudder ran through her at the memory.

"He'll be all right."

"You're awfully sure of yourself, Mr. . . . ?"

"Fargo," he supplied his name. "Skye Fargo."

"Really?" She sounded surprised. "I think I've heard of you."

"You didn't tell me your name," Fargo reminded her.

"It's Isabel Sterling."

"Pleased to meet you, Miss Sterling. Wish it had been under better circumstances. Like across a poker table."

He heard her sharply indrawn breath. "How did you know I'm a gambler?"

"Your hands, mostly. They look like they'd be good with cards. You're young and beautiful and well dressed, not your everyday riverboat passenger. I reckon maybe you could have a different profession, but you don't strike me as that type."

She gave a short laugh. "I suppose I should be grateful you don't think I'm a harlot."

"So I'm right about you being a gambler?"

"You're right," she admitted.

Fargo had seen quite a few lovely young women who worked the salons of the Mississippi riverboats as gamblers. Men didn't mind losing their money quite so much when they lost it to a lovely young woman. They figured they had gotten the pleasure of her company out of the game, anyway.

It was a little unusual to see a woman as striking as Isabel Sterling in a place like this, though. Even though there was steady riverboat traffic on Big Cypress Bayou, Fargo doubted that there were many high rollers among the passengers. Isabel could have made a lot more money on the Mississippi.

Which meant she probably had a good reason for being here and not there, he reflected.

He pushed that thought aside, since it was really none of his business. Spotting a slight discoloration in the water ahead of the boat, he turned the wheel to send the vessel slipping past it on the right. When they went by, he saw that he was right—a sandbar lurked just below the surface.

"That was pretty good," Isabel said. "Maybe you *have* done this before."

Fargo looked at the unconscious Captain Russell and wondered if he ought to push the boat to a faster speed. The engines could take more, easily. But it wouldn't help Russell any if he ripped the boat's hull open on a snag that he hadn't seen until it was too late.

Isabel rested a hand on Russell's shoulder to steady him as the boat chugged along the bayou. Fargo avoided another sandbar and several dead trees that had fallen in the water to become potentially hazardous snags. He spotted smoke rising into the sky ahead and knew they had to be getting close to Jefferson. A few minutes later the boat rounded a bend as the bayou made a turn to the southwest, and the settlement appeared up ahead.

A dozen or more wharves lined the northern bank of the bayou, which widened out into a broad basin where riverboats could turn around to start the return trip to New Orleans. Several streets ran northwest from the waterfront, and numerous other streets crossed them. Jefferson was already a good-sized town, and it grew larger with each passing month due to the river traffic, the demand for cotton, and the burgeoning timber industry.

"Slow to a quarter!" Fargo called into the speaking tube as he turned the wheel and sent the boat toward the wharves. Another riverboat was tied up at Jefferson's waterfront, but he thought there was plenty of room to move in behind it.

"Don't wreck us," Isabel cautioned.

"I'll try not to," Fargo replied with a tight smile. To tell the truth, he didn't have much experience docking these big vessels. None, in fact. But it *looked* easy enough. . . .

Captain Russell roused from his stupor just then, lifting his head and looking around. He saw the wharf approaching and muttered, "What the hell?" Lurching to his feet, he lifted his good arm and got hold of the speaking tube. "Reverse engines!"

The boat shuddered as down below, Caleb Thorn obeyed the order and threw the twin engines that powered the paddle wheel into reverse. Fargo heard timbers creaking as the big wheel came to a stop and then started turning the other direction. That slowed the vessel's forward progress.

"Stop engines!" Russell called after a moment. He leaned against the blood-spattered chart table and said to Fargo, "Whoever you are, mister, turn that wheel hard aport! That'll swing our stern around and get us lined up right."

Fargo did as he was told, putting some muscle behind it as he spun the wheel and the rudder responded. With only one arm that he could use, Captain Russell wouldn't have been able to turn the wheel far enough or fast enough.

But with the captain telling him what to do, Fargo eased the riverboat up next to the wharf as the vessel drifted to a stop. Caleb Thorn, spry despite his years and the peg leg, leaped from the deck onto the bank, taking a heavy line with him that he looped around a piling and made fast. The boat was tied up now and wouldn't float away on the bayou.

Fargo blew out his breath in a sigh of relief.

"As fast as you were going, you would've rammed us right into the wharf," Russell said with a frown. "Say, aren't you the fella who was working on my arm?"

Isabel spoke up. "That's right, Captain. If not for Mr. Fargo, you'd have bled to death."

"Well, I'm obliged for that, I reckon." He reached over and rubbed his left elbow. "I can't feel this arm."

"That's why you need to get to a doctor right away," Fargo told him. "Those bullet holes in your arm ought to be stitched up before the tourniquet's taken off."

Russell nodded. "Yeah, I suppose you're right." He was a chunky man of about fifty, with iron gray hair and a weathered, clean-shaven face. As he extended his right hand, he went on. "Thanks for your help, Mr. . . . Fargo, was it?"

"That's right," Fargo said as he shook hands with the captain. "Skye Fargo."

Once again the light of recognition appeared in someone's eyes as Fargo mentioned his name. Having a reputation could be both good and bad, Fargo had discovered during his years of wandering. Sometimes he thought a little more anonymity would be nice, but it was too late to worry about that now.

Russell started toward the door of the wheelhouse but weaved suddenly. A wave of weakness and dizziness from losing so much blood must have struck him. Fargo grasped the captain's uninjured arm to steady him. "Come on," Fargo said. "I'll give you a hand."

He went down the short, steep flight of steps to the top of the passenger deck first, then reached up to assist Russell. Isabel Sterling followed close behind the captain. Together they got Russell down to the main deck, and by the time they did, Caleb Thorn had pulled a wide gangplank across to the shore. Fargo walked down it at Russell's side, his arm around the riverboat man's waist.

The boat's arrival had drawn a crowd, as such things nearly always did in river-port towns. A portly man in a tweed suit and a beaver hat pushed forward and said to Russell, "Good Lord, Andy, what happened?"

"Red Mike and his bunch hit us a few miles down the bayou," Russell said. "I stopped a bullet."

The man looked past Russell at the crates stacked on the main deck and said, "They didn't get your cargo, I see."

Russell gave a weak shake of his head. "They never boarded us. Mr. Fargo here came along and chased them off."

The man's eyes widened in surprise as he turned his attention to Fargo. "You chased off Red Mike McShane and his pirates? Good work, sir!"

Fargo nodded curtly and said, "I appreciate that, but we really need to get Captain Russell here to a doctor. That arm of his needs medical attention."

"Of course." The portly man turned to the crowd and said, "Polton! Cross! Help the captain over to Dr. Fearn's office."

The two men, who appeared to be laborers of some sort, hurried to obey the order. They got on either side of the captain and looped his good arm over the shoulders of one man while the other put his arm around Russell's waist. They half carried him through the crowd, which parted to give them room.

The portly man turned to Isabel then and said, "Hello, Miss Sterling. It's always good to have your gracious presence visiting Jefferson again."

Isabel nodded and said, "Mr. Kiley." Her voice was cool, and she didn't seem to be all that fond of the man, Fargo thought.

The portly man turned back to Fargo, extended his hand, and introduced himself. "Lawrence Kiley, sir. I'm pleased to make your acquaintance."

"Skye Fargo."

"You were on the *Bayou Princess* when she was attacked?"

The question puzzled Fargo for a second until he glanced at the riverboat and saw the name BAYOU PRINCESS painted in neat letters on its bow. He shook his head and said, "No, I was riding through the woods when I heard a bunch of shots and figured I'd better see what the trouble was. Sounded almost like a war."

Kiley's face turned grim as he nodded. "That's pretty much what it is, Mr. Fargo. A war."

"I reckon this isn't the first time those river pirates have attacked a steamboat."

Kiley shook his head. "Not hardly. Red Mike McShane and his brother and the rest of their gang have become a plague on this part of the country."

Fargo might have asked Kiley to tell him more, but at that moment the sound of a horse neighing made him look around. The Ovaro stood on the bayou's far bank, having reached the settlement after following the stream from the place where Fargo had boarded the boat.

"I hope there's a bridge or a ford somewhere around here, so I can get that big fella on this side of the bayou."

"There's a bridge just below the settlement, where the stream gets narrower," Kiley said.

"Obliged for the information," Fargo said with a nod. "I'll go fetch him."

As he turned away, Isabel Sterling stopped him with a light touch of her hand on his arm. "Thank you for everything, Mr. Fargo," she said. "I know I was a little sharp with you a couple of times, but I was upset and worried about Captain Russell."

Fargo smiled at her. "That's all right. I understand. It's a mite bothersome when folks start shooting at me, too."

"I'll be staying at the Excelsior House. Why don't you have dinner with me there this evening?"

Fargo nodded in acceptance of the invitation. "I'd like that," he said as he reached up and tugged on his broad-brimmed brown hat. "I'll see you then, Miss Sterling."

The crowd had begun to thin. Kiley snapped his fingers and spoke to some of the workers, who began unloading the crates of cargo from the *Bayou Princess*'s deck. Fargo had Kiley pegged as a merchant or some other sort of businessman and wondered briefly if the man owned one or more of the big, warehouselike buildings that bulked along the waterfront. That seemed likely, the way Kiley was taking charge.

Fargo walked for several blocks along the waterfront, then spotted the bridge up ahead. It was built out of timbers and was wide enough and sturdy enough to allow wagons to travel over it. He walked across it, and by the time he reached the other side, the Ovaro had trotted up to meet him. The stallion bumped his nose against Fargo's shoulder.

Taking the reins, Fargo turned to lead the stallion back across the bridge, but as he did so he saw several rough-looking men step onto the other end of the span. They stood there glaring at him, blocking his way as if they were daring him to cross.

Fargo stopped, his eyes narrowing. He had never seen these men before, but judging from their powerful builds and the heavy work boots they wore, along with thick canvas overalls and woolen shirts, he thought they were probably loggers. He had seen such men before, in the forests of the Pacific Northwest.

They didn't look a bit friendly, either.

One of them stepped ahead of the others—a tall man with several days' worth of beard stubble on his heavy jaw. He rumbled, "So you're a friend o' Russell's and Kiley's."

"I never met either of them before today," Fargo said.

The man spat off the side of the bridge and said, as if he hadn't even heard Fargo's answer, "Any friend o' those bastards is a bastard, too."

He stalked forward with his big knuckled hands clenched into malletlike fists, obviously intent on a fight.

Fargo dropped the Ovaro's reins and said, "Hold on there, hombre. I'm not looking for a fight."

"You should've thought of that before you threw in with Russell and Kiley," the man grated. Then with a roar of rage, he charged straight at Fargo.

The man appeared to be unarmed, so Fargo didn't reach for his Colt or the Arkansas toothpick that rode in a fringed sheath strapped to his leg. Instead he stood his ground until his attacker was almost on top of him, swinging a roundhouse punch that would have taken Fargo's head off if it had connected.

Fargo didn't let it connect. He ducked under the whistling fist and stepped aside. The man stumbled past him, thrown off balance by the missed punch and his own momentum. Fargo sliced the side of his right hand against the back of the man's neck in a short but powerful blow that finished the job. The man pitched forward to slam face-first into the planks of the bridge.

His companions yelled indignant curses and thundered across the span toward Fargo. Outnumbered four to one, he did the only sensible thing.

He palmed the Colt from its holster and lifted it, earing back the hammer as the barrel came level. The men charging toward him all skidded to a stop as they found themselves staring down the barrel of the heavy revolver.

"I realize you boys aren't packing irons," Fargo said, "but I'll be damned if I'm going to just stand here and let you beat the hell out of me because of that."

A couple of the men swallowed hard. Their faces had gone pale under the tans that working outside had given them. "Take it easy, mister," one of them said in a nervous voice. "Nobody has to get killed here."

"That's what I was thinking," Fargo said. "Now back off of this bridge and let me pass, and maybe we'll forget about what happened here. I don't know what your grudge is against Russell and Kiley, but it's got nothing to do with me."

The men started to back up, and Fargo reached for the Ovaro's reins. But before he could grasp them, he heard the scrape of leather on wood and twisted part of the way around to see that the first man had recovered from being stunned and climbed back to his feet. Blood streamed from his nose, which had been pulped by the impact when he landed on it.

But that didn't stop him from throwing himself at Fargo with a strangled curse. He smashed into the Trailsman, and Fargo felt himself falling as the man tackled him around the waist.

3

The impact as Fargo crashed down on the bridge with his attacker on top of him drove all the air from his lungs. He gasped for breath and balls of red-and-black fire danced before his eyes as he struggled not to lose consciousness. Aware that his furious opponents might kick and stomp him to death if he stayed down, he struck upward with all the strength he could muster at the man who had him pinned to the bridge.

The blow caught the man in the beard-stubbled jaw and rocked him back. Fargo caught hold of the front of the man's overalls, arched his back, and rolled and heaved. The man was thrown off him, and as Fargo came over onto his belly, he saw the man disappear off the side of the bridge. A second later, a big splash told Fargo that the man had landed in the bayou.

Fargo didn't have time to feel any particular triumph about that. The others were all around him as he surged to his feet. Fists smashed into him, sending heavy jolts through his body. But he stayed upright and fought back. He had dropped his gun when the first man tackled him, but he still had his fists.

He slammed a punch into the middle of a man's face, then bent to the side and snapped a kick into another man's midsection. That bought him a little room, but the respite lasted only a split second, just long enough for Fargo to drag in a breath. Then one of the other men landed on his back and tried to loop an arm around his throat.

Fargo leaned forward, reached back, grabbed a double handful of hair, and hauled the man over the top of his own back. The hombre screeched in pain as some of his hair was ripped out by the roots. The yell stopped abruptly as the man crashed down on his back.

Fargo stepped away from him and whirled around, fists up and ready to do battle against the remaining attacker. That man had other problems at the moment, however. He yelped in alarm and went diving off the side of the bridge to avoid the Ovaro's iron-shod hooves. The stallion had reared up and danced forward, lashing out with his hooves and forcing the man to flee.

With two of his enemies in the bayou and the other three sprawled on the bridge, stunned and battered, Fargo took the opportunity to pick up the gun he had dropped a moment earlier. The fight, violent though it had been, hadn't really lasted very long.

He covered the three men as he picked up his hat, too, and put it on. He said, "I told you I wasn't looking for trouble. Too bad you boys didn't believe me."

One of the men pushed himself into a sitting position and flinched as the Ovaro turned toward him, nostrils flaring. "Keep that devil horse away from us!" he said. "I reckon you win this battle, mister, but the war ain't over yet!"

"In that case, I'd be better off killing you now, wouldn't I?" Fargo asked in a cold, dangerous voice.

The man gulped and started scooting away. "That'd be murder!"

"And what would it have been if the five of you had stomped me to death?"

"We wouldn't have done that," the man answered in a surly voice. "All we were gonna do was rough you up a mite, so you wouldn't go to work for Kiley."

"Nobody's offered me a job, and I'm not looking for one," Fargo snapped. "Next time don't jump to conclusions."

Leading the stallion, he walked past the men and off the bridge on the settlement side of the bayou. The man who had attacked him first climbed out of the stream, and with water dripping from him, he yelled after Fargo, "This ain't over yet, you son of a bitch!"

The insult made Fargo think about going back and continuing the fight, but in the end he kept walking, because the effort wasn't worth it.

Besides, if the man was telling the truth, Fargo figured he would get another chance to square things.

In the meantime, he looked for a livery barn, and when he found one, he took the Ovaro inside and rented a stall from the proprietor, a middle-aged Mexican with a paunch and a friendly grin.

As he unsaddled the stallion, Fargo asked the man, "Where will I find the Excelsior House?"

"It's around the corner on Austin Street. You can't miss it. Nicest place in town."

That was appropriate for Isabel Sterling, Fargo thought. A woman like her deserved a nice place to stay.

"I saw some of that fandango down at the bridge," the liveryman went on. "What'd you do to get Nick Dirkson mad at you?"

"Big fella, got a jaw like a shovel?"

The man nodded. "That's him, all right."

"He was upset because he thought I was friends with that fella Kiley, or working for him or something."

"Oh. That explains it, then."

"Explains what?" Fargo wanted to know.

The stable keeper raised both hands, palms out, and backed away. "I got to live here and do business here," he said. "So I stay out of it."

Fargo saw that he wasn't going to get any answers from the man, so he dug a coin out of his pocket, flipped it to him, and said, "See that my horse is taken good care of."

"Now that I can do," the man said with a grin as he plucked the coin from the air.

Fargo left the barn, taking his saddlebags and Henry rifle with him, and walked up to the corner, where he turned onto Austin Street and immediately spied the Excelsior House, as the stableman had said that he would. The hotel took up most of a block. It was two stories tall and built of whitewashed bricks and timbers. A second-floor balcony bordered with a fancy wrought-iron railing ran along the front of the building. The Excelsior House looked like it had been constructed fairly recently, and it was the nicest place in town, also as the liveryman had said.

Two sets of double doors led into the lobby. Fargo went inside through the left-hand pair. Ahead of him was the arched entrance to the dining room. The desk was to the right, and beyond it the staircase that led to the second floor. Several large windows made the lobby bright and airy. There were nice rugs on the floor and potted plants tucked into the corners of the room.

Fargo went to the desk and said to the man who stood behind it wearing a frock coat, "I'd like a room, and I'm supposed to meet Miss Isabel Sterling here for dinner, too."

The clerk eyed Fargo's buckskins with a rather dubious gaze until Fargo slapped a gold double eagle on the counter. Then the man smiled and said, "Of course, sir. If you'll just sign in . . ." He turned the register toward Fargo and added, "Or make your mark."

Fargo grunted and reined in the irritation he felt at the implication that he might not be able to read or write. He dipped the pen in the inkwell and signed his name in the register. The clerk raked in the double eagle and took a key from a peg board on the wall behind him.

"I'll put you in room eight," he said. "That's right across the hall from Miss Sterling."

Fargo started to say that it wasn't necessary for him and Isabel to be in such close proximity, but then he changed his mind. No point in arguing with fate, he thought.

He carried his gear, what little there was of it, upstairs and put it in the room, which was furnished with a comfortable-looking four-poster bed with a ruffled yellow spread. A dressing table had a basin of fresh water on it, so Fargo stripped off his buckskin shirt, washed up, and put on a fresh shirt from his saddlebags. After running his fingers through his damp hair, he went across the hall to knock on the door of room seven, which was located on the front side of the hotel.

Isabel had changed clothes, too, he saw as she opened the door a moment later. Now she wore a lighter blue dress with a curved neckline bordered by delicate white lace. Her hair was pinned up in a slightly different arrangement. A gold locket hung from a necklace and nestled at the top of the cleft between her full breasts.

"Hello, Mr. Fargo," she said. "Did you have any trouble finding the hotel?"

"Not a bit," he replied, without adding that the only trouble he'd had was getting here past those loggers who'd wanted to thrash him. "I didn't know if you were ready for supper or not."

"Yes, I am. It's been a long day and I was thinking about turning in early tonight." She stepped away from the door. "Just let me get my shawl."

Fargo waited as she picked up a lace shawl and draped it around her shoulders, making her look even lovelier. He took her arm to escort her downstairs.

"Have you heard anything about how Captain Russell is doing?" he asked as they descended the stair-case.

"Yes, Mr. Kiley stopped by to let me know that the captain should be all right. He'll be staying at Dr. Fearn's for a few days, though, while he recuperates."

"That means the riverboat won't be going back down the bayou for a while," Fargo said.

"No, I'm afraid not." Isabel frowned. "The captain's already had a great deal of trouble keeping crew members on the *Bayou Princess* because men are afraid of Red Mike McShane. This latest attack is just going to make things worse."

They reached the lobby and turned to go into the dining room, where round tables were laid with pris-tine white cloths and glittering silver. A pair of crystal chandeliers lit the room. Outside, dusk was settling over Jefferson, but the dining room of the Excelsior House was filled with a warm glow.

Most of the tables were occupied by men in suits. They were drummers or other sorts of businessmen, Fargo thought. And they all had appreciative glances for Isabel as she and Fargo found a vacant table and sat down. There were a few other women in the room, but Isabel was easily the most attractive female here.

A waitress in a starched white apron brought coffee to the table and took their order. While they were waiting for their food, the clerk from the lobby came over and bent to say quietly to Fargo, "I heard that there was some trouble this afternoon, sir, with Mr. Dirkson and his friends. There's not going to be any, uh, recurrence of that, is there? The Excelsior discour-ages brawling among its guests."

Again Fargo felt a surge of irritation. This fella just rubbed him the wrong way. "I don't go looking for trouble," he said. "But I'm not in the habit of running away from it, either."

The clerk pursed his lips. He was a skinny man with wispy fair hair and spectacles perched on his rather long nose. "Very well," he said. "I suppose that will have to do."

As the clerk returned to the lobby, Isabel leaned forward and asked Fargo, "What was that all about? You got in a fight with Nick Dirkson?"

"I reckon you must know who he is."

She nodded. "He's Jonas Baxter's foreman, and a bad man to have for an enemy. It's rumored that he's beaten men to death with his bare hands."

Fargo could believe that. Dirkson looked brutal enough to do such a thing. He asked, "Who's Jonas Baxter?"

"The owner of the second-largest logging operation around here."

"And the biggest one belongs to?"

"Mr. Kiley."

"Ah." Things were starting to make more sense to Fargo now. "What's the connection between Kiley and Captain Russell?"

"Mr. Kiley has an exclusive contract with the captain to transport logs over to the sawmills in Shreveport. That's the extent of it, though. They're not exactly partners or anything like that. Mr. Kiley *has* similar contracts with several of the riverboat captains."

"But this Jonas Baxter resents the fact that Russell won't do business with him," Fargo guessed.

Isabel shrugged. "Jonas Baxter resents everything about Mr. Kiley's operation, as far as I can tell. And Mr. Kiley *has* tried to make it more difficult for Baxter to get his logs downstream to the mills. He's a sharp businessman and looks for every advantage he can get."

Fargo understood now. Baxter's hostility toward Kiley was shared by the men who worked for him, naturally enough. Dirkson and the others, seeing that Fargo had lent a hand to Captain Russell and helped bring in the *Bayou Princess*, had decided that he might be tied in with Kiley like Russell was. That explained their grudge against him and why they had picked a fight with him.

"Where does McShane come in?" he asked.

Isabel looked puzzled. "You mean Red Mike? He doesn't have any connection with any of the logging outfits. He's just a river pirate. He and his men have held up several of the boats in the past few months."

Fargo nodded, but he found himself wondering if that was all there was to it. According to what Isabel had said earlier, Russell was having trouble keeping crewmen because they were afraid of McShane's gang. It would be interesting to know whether the other boats that had been attacked by McShane were also vessels with exclusive contracts to transport Lawrence Kiley's timber. Anything that made life more difficult for Kiley would ultimately be to the benefit of his chief competitor, Jonas Baxter. That was the way it seemed to Fargo, anyway.

When you came right down to it, though, he told himself, none of this was any of his business. He hadn't been headed anywhere in particular when he heard the shots that afternoon, and he had no stake in what was going on here in Jefferson. Come morning, he could saddle up the Ovaro and ride away without looking back.

The waitress arrived with their food, and the meal was excellent, reminding Fargo that Jefferson, despite its rather isolated location, was one of the most important cities in Texas. Folks here were used to treating visitors right.

When they had finished eating and were lingering over cups of coffee, Isabel asked, "How long do you plan to stay here, Mr. Fargo?"

"First of all, call me Skye," he suggested with a smile. "And I don't have any plans."

"I've heard that you work as a wagon train guide and a scout for the army, things like that."

He nodded. "Sometimes. But I don't have any chores lined up right now, so I'm just drifting. Seeing what's on the other side of the hill." He smiled. "That's a weakness of mine."

"You won't find many hills in this part of the country. The terrain is pretty flat."

"On the other side of the trees, then."

"Now *those* you'll find plenty of."

Fargo knew what she meant. Jefferson was located toward the northern end of what was sometimes called the Big Thicket, a band of forest that stretched all the way down nearly to the Gulf of Mexico. Longleaf, shortleaf, and loblolly pines dominated the woodlands, but cypress, beech, magnolia, oak, and hickory trees could also be found here in abundance. That was why logging had become such an important industry in recent years, growing until it rivaled the production of cotton.

East Texas, with its thick forests, swamps, oppressive heat in the summer, dampness all year-round, and mosquitoes that the locals bragged were big enough to carry off a small dog, wasn't one of Fargo's favorite places. He liked the high plains and the mountains farther west and spent most of his time out there.

But his restless nature kept him on the move, and sometimes he found himself in places like this. He was the sort of man who could find something to enjoy about almost anywhere, and he had to admit that the piney woods had a few good features, not the least of which was the crisp, sweet scent of the trees. Flowers bloomed in wild profusion most of the year, too, and the landscape was splashed with brilliant color because of it. The Spanish moss that draped many of the cypress trees along the bayous was striking, too.

And of course, here and now in Jefferson, the company of Isabel Sterling was quite an attraction, too. She was a quick-witted, intelligent young woman in addition to being beautiful, and Fargo enjoyed talking to her. When they finished with their meal, he linked arms with her again and walked her back upstairs.

Isabel had commented that she intended to go to bed early, so Fargo thought that after he bid her good night he might stroll around town, maybe find a saloon where he could get a good drink of whiskey and a friendly poker game. He was still wide-awake, and that sounded like a decent way to spend the evening.

When they paused in front of Isabel's door, though, she turned to him with a smile and asked, "Would you like to come in, Skye?"

"I thought you said you planned on turning in early," he commented.

The smile spread to her eyes, where it took on a mischievous sparkle. "I do," she said as she rested her hands lightly on his chest, "but I never said anything about going to bed alone, now, did I?"

4

Fargo returned the smile, cupped his hand under Isabel's chin, and tilted her head back a little as he brought his mouth down on hers. He had been attracted to her as soon as he saw her, and evidently the feeling was mutual.

Her lips were soft and warm and tasted sweet. The kiss was gentle at first, their mouths barely brushing against each other, but as Isabel slid her hands down to his waist and leaned against him so that her breasts pressed into his chest, the kiss became more urgent. Fargo's tongue stroked her lips, and they parted, eager to invite him in.

Fargo accepted the invitation, delving into the hot, wet cavern of her mouth. Her tongue met his in a sensuous duel as they swirled and circled around each other. Isabel locked her arms around Fargo's waist and molded her body to his. He moved his hands to her back and slid them down to the swelling curve of her rump.

His manhood grew hard, and she had to feel it pressing against the softness of her belly. She pressed forward with her hips, grinding herself into him. The passion they had kindled within each other roared up into a fierce, all-consuming blaze.

After a few moments, Isabel pulled back a little and said, "We probably shouldn't be standing out here in the hall doing this, Skye. Why don't you come inside with me?"

Fargo chuckled. "I thought you'd never ask."

Isabel slipped out of his embrace, turned, and unlocked the door. She had left the lamp on the bedside table burning, Fargo saw as he followed her into the room, with its flame turned down so that it gave off only a faint glow.

But that was enough to see by as he closed the door behind them and she started taking off her clothes.

He watched with great appreciation as she pulled the top of the dress down, baring her shoulders and the upper part of her breasts. She reached behind her to unfasten the buttons on the back of the dress, which made her breasts stand out even more. As the buttons came free, the dress slid more. Isabel shrugged it off, along with the shift she wore under it. She pushed the garments down around her waist.

Her breasts were high and firm and full, creamy young mounds of womanhood crowned with large, pale pink nipples that cried out for a man's tongue to lick them. She cupped her breasts in her palms and ran her thumbs over the nipples, making them grow hard. The erect buds were even more appealing.

Fargo resisted the temptation, though. He was made of sterner stuff than most men. With a faint smile on his face, he waited for her to finish disrobing. Isabel pushed dress and shift and petticoats down over her hips and let them fall to the floor around her feet. She kicked them away, along with her slippers, and that left her clad only in white cotton stockings that came up just over her knees.

"Now you, Skye," she whispered in a husky voice.

Fargo unbuckled his gun belt, coiled it around the holstered Colt, and placed it on a chair beside the bed where it would be within easy reach. That was habit on his part. His adventurous life had taught him it was always wise to have a weapon handy.

32

He unstrapped the sheathed Arkansas toothpick from his leg and set it on the dressing table. Then he pulled the buckskin shirt over his head, revealing his broad, muscular chest that was lightly matted with dark brown hair.

"Let me get your boots," Isabel offered.

Fargo sat down on the edge of the bed and stuck out his right leg. Isabel turned her back to him and straddled it, leaning over to grasp the high-topped black boot and pull it off his foot. Considering that she was nude except for her stockings, that position provided Fargo with quite an intriguing view. Isabel had to know that, and he suspected that was one reason she had offered to help him remove the boots.

She repeated the process with the left boot, then turned and came close to the bed, standing there in front of Fargo. He took advantage of the opportunity to lean forward and close his lips around the nipple of her left breast. He ran his tongue around the bud of erect flesh and then sucked gently on it. Isabel sighed in pleasure as she rested her hands on his head and stroked her fingers through his thick dark hair.

Fargo gave equal attention to the nipple on the right breast. Then Isabel knelt before him and said, "Lift your hips." When he did so, she slipped her hands into the waistband of the buckskin trousers and pulled them down over his thighs, along with his long-handled underwear. His erection sprang free, jutting up from the thicket of dark hair at its base.

Isabel tossed the trousers and underwear aside and then leaned forward to close both hands around his long, thick shaft. She stroked it up and down, and the soft touch of her palms made Fargo groan. He clenched his jaw to prevent an even louder response as her tongue made a heated swipe all the way up the underside of the shaft from its base to its crown. When she reached the top, she pressed her lips to it in a kiss.

Her oral caresses continued for long, maddening

moments until it was all Fargo could do not to explode down her throat. Perhaps sensing this, Isabel drew back and stood up. Fargo eased back on the bed, and she straddled him, placing a knee on either side of his hips as she poised herself above the iron-hard pole of his manhood.

As soon as Fargo felt the searing touch of her opening, he grasped her hips, pulling her down and thrusting up at the same time. She gasped in delight as his member sheathed itself inside her, filling the hot, clasping vault of her femininity. "Oh, God, Skye!" she whispered. "I never . . . I never . . ."

She couldn't go on, because he had reached up with his left hand to cup her right breast and slipped his right hand down where they were joined to rub the sensitive spot at the top of her sex. Isabel took short, sharp breaths as her climax shuddered through her.

Fargo was far from finished with her. He remained inside her as she lay forward to rest on his chest as her culmination trailed away. She was breathing hard and he felt her heart pounding. He let her rest like that for a few minutes, lightly stroking her flanks as he did so, but then he began moving his hips a little so that his shaft slid in and out of her, an inch or so at a time.

That began to increase Isabel's arousal again. She started pumping her hips to meet Fargo's thrusts. After a moment she rested her hands on his chest and pushed herself into a sitting position again. She took Fargo's hands and brought them to her breasts, urging him to squeeze and caress the firm globes. His thumbs strummed the hard nipples as she rode him in an ever-quickening pace.

Fargo waited until her eyes were closed and he could tell that she was on the verge of erupting in another climax. Then he grasped her hips in a tight grip and rolled over, remaining buried inside her as he put himself on top. His hips thrust forward as he finally unleashed his own passion and made love to her with a hard, driving urgency.

Isabel wrapped her arms around his neck and her legs around his waist as he pounded into her. She moaned in his ear. As she began spasming in culmination again, Fargo's climax surged up, too. He exploded inside her, filling her with burst after burst of his scalding juices.

The moment seemed to go on forever but finally came to a shuddering end. Fargo would have rolled off so that his weight wouldn't be crushing Isabel, but she held him so tightly that it seemed she never wanted to let him go.

At last she sighed and said, "That was incredible, Skye. I knew that if we ever got together, it would be good, but I didn't expect it to be *that* good."

Fargo withdrew from her and rolled onto his side, propping himself up on an elbow so that he could look down into her flushed but still lovely face. "Sometimes people are lucky," he said. "They're in the right place at the right time to meet someone, and everything comes together."

"So to speak," she said with an impish grin.

Fargo laughed. "Yeah. So to speak."

Her face grew more serious as she went on. "But that doesn't mean those moments will last, does it? People move on."

"Some people do," Fargo admitted.

"And you're not the sort of man who stays any place for very long."

"I never have been before . . . but I'm here now."

She reached up and rested the palm of her hand against his cheek. "I know," she whispered. "And that's going to have to be enough. I understand that. But . . . you'll stay with me tonight, Skye?"

"I'm not going anywhere," Fargo said in a voice rough with emotion, "as long as you want me here."

"Oh, I want you," Isabel said. She slipped her hand

behind Fargo's head so she could pull his mouth down to hers. "I want you very much," she whispered just before their lips met again.

That night, Fargo never did make it to one of Jefferson's saloons for that drink and poker game. Instead he spent it in Isabel's bed as they explored every inch of each other's bodies again and again, finally dozed off in exhaustion, woke up and made love again, and then drifted back into slumber.

Fargo woke up early enough the next morning to slip out of bed, get dressed, and return to his own room across the hall before anybody else was up and around. No point in scandalizing that prissy clerk, he thought . . . although it might have been entertaining to watch the hombre's reaction if he knew that Fargo had spent the night with Isabel.

Fargo stretched out on his own bed and slept for a while longer, and as a result, the sun was already up by the time he woke again. That was unusual for him. Like most frontiersmen, he was in the habit of being an early riser.

He splashed water on his face, got dressed, and went downstairs. When he walked into the dining room he looked around, thinking that Isabel might be there having breakfast. He didn't see her anywhere, but Lawrence Kiley was seated at one of the tables. Kiley caught Fargo's eye, raised a hand, and motioned him over.

Kiley waved a hand at the empty chair on the other side of the table and said, "Won't you join me, Mr. Fargo?" The remains of a hearty breakfast were in front of the man, but he still had a half-full cup of coffee.

"Don't mind if I do." Fargo pulled out the chair and sat down, dropping his hat on the floor beside him.

The waitress brought a cup and a fresh pot of coffee without being asked. Fargo ordered flapjacks, bacon, and hash browns, then poured himself some coffee and took an appreciative sip of the hot, strong brew.

"I've already been by Dr. Fearn's this morning to check on poor Captain Russell," Kiley said.

"How's he doing?" Fargo asked.

"As well as can be expected. He's as weak as a kitten because of all the blood he lost, but he'll recover from that. And of course his wounded arm is still causing him quite a bit of pain. The bullet did enough damage to the muscles that the doctor says it could be weeks or even months before Andy recovers his full strength in that arm."

Fargo frowned. "That's going to make it sort of hard for him to handle that steamboat, isn't it?"

"I'm afraid so," Kiley replied with a sigh. "It'll be a week or so before he's strong enough to get around much, Dr. Fearn says, and he'll have to have a good helmsman to handle the wheel before the *Bayou Princess* can start back downstream." Kiley regarded Fargo with interest. "Would you be interested in the job, Mr. Fargo?"

Fargo grinned and shook his head. "I managed to help get that boat here yesterday, but I'm afraid I'm not cut out for that chore."

"Well, maybe I can find somebody else," Kiley said with a shrug. He changed the subject by continuing, "I heard you had a run-in with Nick Dirkson after you got here yesterday."

Fargo nodded. "Yeah, he and some of his friends saw me with you and Captain Russell and got it in their heads that we were friends."

"I hope we will be."

"Dirkson didn't want me going to work for you," Fargo went on. "They thought roughing me up might scare me off."

"Obviously they didn't know who you are, or they wouldn't have tried such a thing."

The waitress arrived with Fargo's food. He always

had a healthy appetite, so he dug in with gusto for a few minutes before resuming the conversation with Kiley.

"I'm curious about this river pirate, McShane," Fargo said. "I'm told he and his men have attacked several of the boats that travel on Big Cypress Bayou. Were those other boats ones that carry your timber to Shreveport for you?"

"As a matter of fact, they were." Kiley leaned forward with a frown on his round florid face. "You think that was a coincidence, Mr. Fargo?"

Fargo responded to that question with another of his own. "Have any boats carrying logs for Jonas Baxter been hit?"

Kiley shook his head. "Not even once. And I must say, I'm glad that someone besides me finally finds that a little suspicious."

"I hear Captain Russell is having trouble keeping a crew because of McShane. What about the other captains?"

"They're having the same problem. I used to ship two or three loads a week down the bayou. Now I'm lucky if I can get one load to the mills every week."

"Have you talked to the law about McShane?"

Kiley grimaced. "Sheriff Higgins does a good job of keeping the peace here in Jefferson, but he claims he can't spend his time chasing around the swamps and the sloughs looking for McShane. My feeling is that Baxter got to him and convinced him not to try too hard to find those pirates. I hate to accuse anyone of being corrupt, but . . ." His face suddenly lit up. "Say! I know you don't want to work on the riverboat, Mr. Fargo, but what would you say to the job of tracking down McShane and his river rats? If you could stop them from plaguing my shipments, it would be worth a lot to me . . . and I'd make it worth your while, too."

Fargo turned the proposal over in his mind. He had gone after outlaw gangs in the past, and this was no different. Besides, even though he hadn't met Jonas Baxter, he didn't like the man because of the run-in with Dirkson and the other loggers, and if there was a connection between Baxter and McShane, Fargo wouldn't mind exposing it.

And he couldn't forget the way the river pirates had attacked the *Bayou Princess* the day before, putting Isabel Sterling's life in danger. Even though he hadn't known Isabel at the time, he sure as hell knew her now, and anger smoldered inside him as he thought about how she might easily have died in that attack.

"I don't have any pressing business elsewhere," he said after mulling it over for a few moments. "I reckon I could stay around here for a while and see what I can turn up."

"That would mean a great deal to me," Kiley said. "I don't mind telling you, Mr. Fargo, things are starting to look a little grim for my operation. I have to get some logs moved, and soon."

"I'll see what I can do," Fargo said with a nod. "If I can locate McShane's hideout and find proof that Baxter is behind the attacks on the riverboats, the sheriff will have to do something about it."

"Indeed, he will," Kiley agreed. Then he looked past Fargo and smiled. "Why, hello, my dear."

Fargo looked around and saw Isabel coming toward the table. He got to his feet.

"Good morning, gentlemen," she said. She smiled at the Trailsman. "You slept well, I hope, Mr. Fargo."

"Very well," Fargo said. "And yourself?"

"Never better."

"I have to be going," Kiley said, "but why don't you join Mr. Fargo for breakfast, Miss Sterling? I'm sure he wouldn't mind the company."

Fargo echoed the invitation and held Isabel's chair for her as she sat down. Kiley put on his beaver hat and said, "I'll talk to you later about that, ah, arrangement, Mr. Fargo."

When Kiley was gone and Fargo was sitting across the table from Isabel, she leaned forward and asked, "What arrangement was he talking about?"

Fargo didn't see any harm in telling her, although he kept his voice low so that no one at any of the other tables would overhear. "I'm going to try to track down McShane and his gang of river pirates. Kiley and I both think there may be some connection between them and Jonas Baxter."

Isabel's perfectly curved eyebrows arched in surprise. "You're going after McShane? That could be dangerous, Skye."

"I plan on being careful," he said with a smile.

"You'd better be. Now that we've met, I don't want anything happening to you." She paused, then said, "I have to admit, even though I'll worry about you trying to find those pirates, I'm glad to know you're going to be staying around here for a while."

"You won't be leaving right away, either," Fargo pointed out. "Kiley told me that it's going to be at least a week before Captain Russell can assume command of that riverboat again, and even then, he's going to need a good helmsman."

"Well, I can think of worse places to spend some time than Jefferson. It's a nice town. There are several decent saloons where I can find a game."

"You plan to gamble?"

"It's how I make my living, Skye, remember?"

Fargo hadn't forgotten. And as pleasant as it had been spending time with Isabel in bed, he had a feeling he would enjoy sitting across a poker table from her, too. She would be a good competitor.

After breakfast, she wanted to go see Andy Russell, so Fargo volunteered to walk with her over to Dr. Fearn's house. He wanted to talk to Russell about the river pirates. Since the captain steamed up and down the bayou on a regular basis, he ought to know the country around here pretty well. Maybe he could give

Fargo an idea of where to start looking for Red Mike McShane.

They left the Excelsior House and started strolling toward the doctor's place. As they made their way, Fargo's instincts warned him that he was being watched. He turned his head quickly and caught a glimpse of a man ducking around a corner into an alley between Austin and Lafayette Streets. Fargo didn't recognize the man and didn't really see anything except a shock of black hair under a battered old hat and a black patch over one eye.

He would know the fella if he ever saw him again, though, and if it became obvious that the one-eyed man was trailing him . . .

Well, in that case, Fargo thought, he would just have to find out *why*.

5

Dr. John Fearn was a gaunt man with white hair, deep-set eyes, and a slight British accent. The accent didn't surprise Fargo. Folks from all over the world wound up on the American frontier.

"Try not to tire him out," Fearn cautioned as he led Fargo and Isabel into a room where Captain Andy Russell sat up in a bed. "He lost a great deal of blood, you know."

Russell grunted and said, "They ought to know. They were right there in the middle of it." He lifted his good arm and held out the hand toward Fargo. "You must be the fella who saved my life. Isabel told me all about it."

Fargo shook hands with the captain. "Skye Fargo," he introduced himself. "And I reckon I just came along at the right time to pitch in and give you a hand."

"If you hadn't, I likely would've bled to death and McShane would've looted all the cargo on my boat. No telling what would have happened to poor Isabel here."

She lifted her chin defiantly. "If those river rats had tried to lay a finger on me, they would've had a fight on their hands."

Russell laughed. "I'll just bet they would have!"

Fargo pulled up chairs for him and Isabel, and they

sat down beside the bed. Russell went on, "I remember a little about what happened after I got hit, but not much. Where'd you come from, Mr. Fargo?"

For the next few minutes, Fargo told the captain about how he had heard the shots as he was riding through the forest and had gone to investigate.

"That was lucky for me and everybody on the *Bayou Princess*," Russell said.

"It certainly was," Isabel agreed, and Fargo thought he saw a faint blush on her face for a moment. She was probably thinking about what had happened between them the night before.

"Skye has agreed to try to track down Red Mike," she said.

Russell turned a surprised gaze toward the Trailsman. "Really? Somebody needs to, because the sheriff they've got here damned sure isn't gonna do it. Excuse my language, Isabel."

"You ought to know by now it doesn't bother me, Captain Andy."

"Yeah, well, that don't give me any excuse not to be a gentleman." Russell turned his attention back to Fargo. "McShane's been making life on the bayou miserable for me and some of the other captains. Anything you can do to stop him will be more than welcome, Mr. Fargo."

"Those other riverboat captains you mentioned . . . they all have contracts with Kiley, don't they?"

"Yeah, come to think of it, they do." Russell frowned. "What are you getting at? You think McShane and his bunch are going after particular boats and leaving the others alone?"

"That's exactly what they're doing, according to what you and Kiley have told me. The question now is why."

"Baxter," the captain breathed with a hostile scowl on his face.

Fargo nodded. "It's a possibility. That's one of the

43

things I intend to find out, along with where McShane and his men are holed up when they're not attacking riverboats. Would you have any ideas about that, Captain?"

Russell frowned in thought for a moment and then said, "We'd just passed Alligator Slough when their canoes showed up behind us yesterday. Chances are they were waiting up in the slough until we'd gone past. But that wouldn't have to mean their hideout's up there somewhere." He shrugged. "Doesn't mean it's not, either."

Fargo nodded. "It's a place to start looking, anyway."

"Be careful," Russell warned. "Red Mike's tricky, and he's meaner'n a snake. That little brother of his isn't much better. They remind me of stories I've heard about Big Harpe and Little Harpe."

Fargo knew what Russell was talking about. The Harpe brothers, Micajah, called Big, and Wiley, known as Little, were before his time, but they were famous—or infamous—for being brutal pirates on the Ohio River some sixty years earlier. Vicious and bloodthirsty by nature, they and their gang had preyed on flatboats traveling up and down the river, looting cargo and murdering the boatmen.

"If the McShanes are like the Harpes, they've got a bloody reputation to live up to," Fargo commented. "Where do I find this Alligator Slough?"

Russell gave Fargo directions to the small, creeklike stream that wound north into the woods from Big Cypress Bayou about five miles east of Jefferson.

Fargo and Isabel chatted for a few more minutes with Russell before Dr. Fearn came into the room and hinted strongly that it would be best for them to let the captain get his rest.

"I'm sorry about stranding you here, Isabel," Russell said as he took her hand with his good hand and squeezed it. "As soon as I'm up and about again, we'll head back to Shreveport."

"Don't worry about anything except getting better, Captain Andy," she told him. She glanced at Fargo, then smiled and added, "I'm fine staying here in Jefferson for a while."

"Oh," Russell said in understanding, with a smile of his own. "All right, then."

As they left the doctor's house, Fargo looked around for the one-eyed man who had seemed to be watching him earlier. He didn't see the man anywhere, but he intended to keep an eye out for him—so to speak.

"Are you really going out to Alligator Slough?" Isabel asked.

"I promised Kiley I'd try to track down Red Mike and his gang," Fargo said.

"And you're a man of your word."

Fargo chuckled. "Seems to be one of my failings."

"All right." She paused and put a hand on his arm. "Be careful, Skye. I know when the time comes you'll be riding on, but I want to make as much of our time together as we can."

Fargo nodded and leaned forward to brush a kiss against her soft cheek. "Me, too," he told her.

With that he headed for the stable to saddle up the Ovaro. He could tell that the stallion was eager to get out on the trail again.

So was Fargo. Settlements had their attractions—whiskey, cards, beautiful women—but at heart, what he really liked best was traveling through an untamed land.

Although there were quite a few towns that had sprung up in East Texas, many sections of it still qualified. As he followed the bayou out of Jefferson, he glanced at the thick woods bordering the stream and knew that in their depths lurked all sorts of natural dangers, such as bears, panthers, and wolves. Venomous snakes, such as the rattler, copperhead, and cottonmouth, were common. The coral snake, whose bite was the most lethal of all, could also be found in the forest. Briars and other spiny plants would rip a man's flesh if he wasn't careful.

And of course, there were the *unnatural* dangers, too, like Red Mike McShane and his gang of river pirates. Fargo had heard it said that man was the most vicious predator on the planet, and considering some of the two-legged varmints he had run into, he didn't doubt that for a second.

But there was beauty mixed in with the danger and death, and Fargo appreciated it as much as he was aware of the other. Giant flowers on drooping stalks festooned some of the trees. The singing of birds filled the air, along with the scent of flowers and rich dark earth and, yes, the underlying hint of decay that was unavoidable in such a damp climate. It was all part of life, and Skye Fargo embraced it wholeheartedly.

The trail ran on the other side of the bayou, so Fargo had to find his own way on this side. That became more difficult as the cypress with their spreading roots and mantle of Spanish moss crowded close to the bank. Back of them were the pines, growing so closely together that they formed an almost solid wall. At times Fargo had to dismount and lead the stallion as he sought out narrow paths that would take them through the woods.

The going was slow, and it was midday before Fargo reached Alligator Slough, although it was difficult to tell that because so little sun penetrated into this hazy green wilderness. He stopped as he came to the stream, which was only about a dozen feet wide and maybe three feet deep. Nothing larger than a canoe could have made it up the slough, which took a twisting course northward through the trees. Fargo lost sight of it in fewer than fifty yards.

That meant if he followed the slough he would be moving pretty much blindly through the forest. He wouldn't be able to see what was around the next bend. He might stumble into the camp of the river pirates before he knew it was there.

But that was a chance he would have to take, he told himself. He had made a promise to Lawrence Kiley, and as Isabel had pointed out, he was a man of his word.

Besides, there were other senses besides sight, and those were keen in Skye Fargo, too.

The cypresses grew too thick along the bank of the slough for the Ovaro to make it through without risking a broken leg among the spreading roots. Fargo looped the reins around the horn, rubbed the stallion's shoulder, and murmured, "Wait here for me, big fella."

He wasn't too worried about someone coming along, finding the black-and-white horse, and trying to capture him. The Ovaro was a one-man horse and could take care of himself. Anyone who got too close to the stallion without Fargo's permission would have to worry about slashing hooves and big, strong teeth taking a wicked bite out of their hide.

Leaving the Ovaro there, where a little grass grew on the bank of the bayou, Fargo set out along Alligator Slough. He jumped from root to root among the cypresses, steadying himself with a hand against the trunks when need be.

He was able to travel fairly fast that way, and it didn't take him long to penetrate several hundred yards into the forest. Something splashed in the water, and as he looked to his right he saw several alligators, each of them five or six feet long, gliding into the slough from the bank. They sank into the stream until only their eyes were visible above the surface as they swam.

Alligator Slough had come by its name honestly,

Fargo thought. That was a good reason to be careful and not fall in. Another was the wriggling black shape of a cottonmouth he spotted in the water, heading away from the gators.

Fargo moved on, twisting and turning along with the slough. The passage of time didn't mean much—when the sun set, the dim light would disappear suddenly, like a candle flame being blown out, but until then, things wouldn't change much. Fargo tried to keep track in his head of how far he had gone and how long it had been since he left the Ovaro, but it was almost impossible to do in these otherworldly surroundings.

He stopped short, lifted his head a little, and sniffed the air. Something new had been added to the mixture of scents, and after a second Fargo caught another whiff of it and identified it. His first thought had been correct.

Wood smoke.

Somebody had a camp near here; the smoke was proof of that. But it might not be the river pirates, Fargo reminded himself. There were probably some fur trappers in these woods, along with alligator hunters. Someone might have even found enough open land to start a small farm, although that was more doubtful.

But it was also possible that he had found McShane's camp, and Fargo pushed on, eager to be sure one way or the other.

His eagerness didn't make him any less careful, though. In fact, he slowed down a bit, just to be certain that he didn't stumble right into the camp.

The smell of smoke grew stronger, and mixed with the scent of burning was that of pipe tobacco. Fargo paused and listened intently for a moment. He heard men's voices, but he couldn't make out the words.

Then he heard something that surprised him: a woman's laugh.

With a frown, Fargo stepped away from the bayou and moved into the pine trees. He began to circle through them. It was his intention to approach the camp from a different direction, rather than following the slough all the way there. He thought his chances of not being spotted would be better that way.

It would be easy to get lost in this trackless forest, though, and wind up going around and around in circles. Fargo concentrated, listening to his senses and his instincts and letting them guide him through the pines. The smoke grew stronger and the voices louder.

The underbrush became so thick that he was forced to get down on his belly and crawl beneath the tangled briars. The ground was carpeted with decades' worth of fallen pine needles and cypress leaves, all of which had rotted together. That made the ground unpleasantly damp, but at least the stuff didn't crackle like dry leaves would have as he crawled over it, Fargo told himself.

He could make out what the men were saying now. Most of the conversation seemed to consist of obscene gibes. Fargo smelled roasting meat and knew from what he overheard that the men were cooking a small hog that one of them had shot earlier in the day. Feral hogs, descendants of animals that had wandered away from farms farther south, were also common here in the thickets.

Fargo moved some brush aside, being careful not to make any noise as he did it, and found himself looking out into a large clearing. It wasn't a natural clearing; the stumps that remained where trees had been hacked down were proof of that. The pines that had been felled had been used to construct several log cabins that sat alongside Alligator Slough.

Fargo counted eight men moving around the cabins and knew there must be more inside, because the gang numbered at least a dozen. One of the men was a big, brawny hombre with coppery hair and a bushy beard of the same shade. Fargo pegged him as Red Mike McShane, although of course that guess could have been wrong. But as he watched from the concealment of the thick brush, Fargo heard the big man giving orders and figured that confirmed McShane's identity.

Another redhead emerged from one of the cabins. He was small and wiry, with a face like a weasel. Despite the difference in sizes, Fargo detected a family resemblance. It looked like the McShane brothers had more in common with the Harpes than just a bloodthirsty nature and a career as river pirates. One was big and one was little.

But then the smaller man said in a sharp voice, "Linus!"

The big red-bearded gent turned around and said, "Yeah, Mike?"

Fargo gave a soft grunt. That would teach him to judge by appearances. The little weaselly hombre was Red Mike, the leader of the gang. That made the big fella his brother and lieutenant, who seemed to be called Linus. Mike probably provided the brains for the river pirates, while Linus enforced his brother's decisions with his brawn.

"We're runnin' short of supplies," Red Mike went on. "I reckon you better go get some. Take Wilcox and Patton with you."

"Sure, Mike," Linus said with a bob of his head.

Fargo asked himself where the men could go to pick up supplies. As notorious river pirates, they couldn't just go into Jefferson and waltz into a general store. Somebody would be too likely to recognize them if they tried that.

A woman emerged from the same cabin Red Mike had come out of. She was buttoning a ragged homespun dress. Her straw-colored hair was a wild tangle. Even though she probably wasn't more than twenty-five years old, judging by the lithe, slender body she possessed, life's hardships had etched a few lines on her face.

Somebody had done worse than that with some sort of blade. An ugly red scar ran from near her left eye down across her cheek to the line of her jaw.

Fargo figured she was Red Mike's woman. He had spotted another woman, older, chunkier, and more slatternly-looking, stirring something in a big iron cooking pot near the fire where the hog roasted on a spit. It wasn't unusual to find a few women in an outlaw hideout. They were prostitutes for the most part, but a few were legally married to the desperadoes they lived with.

Now that Fargo knew where the pirates were holed up, he supposed he could back out of there, retrace his steps to where he had left the Ovaro, and ride back to Jefferson to pass along the information to Sheriff Higgins. Even though he hadn't yet made the acquaintance of the lawman and all he knew about Higgins was what Kiley had told him, he figured no self-respecting badge-toter could ignore being given the location of an outlaw gang that had been plaguing his county.

Fargo wasn't sure what he would do if Higgins *did* refuse to take action against McShane. He had never liked the idea of taking the law into his own hands, but remembering how the likable Captain Andy Russell had almost been killed and how Isabel had been put in danger, too, Fargo knew he might be tempted to do something about the river pirates.

At the moment, however, he couldn't do much of anything, because as he felt something brush against his skin, he looked down to see a small snake with red, yellow, and black bands encircling its body crawling over his left hand.

6

Fargo's breath froze in his throat as he recognized the brightly colored reptile as a coral snake. The red and yellow bands touched each other, which distinguished it from similar-looking but harmless snakes. Fargo lay utterly motionless, knowing that if the snake bit him he would be dead within minutes, and there was nothing he could do about it.

But as if Fargo's hand was nothing more than a broken branch the snake found in its way, it continued to slither across. It cleared his hand and then crawled no more than six inches in front of his face, moving steadily from left to right. Fargo's right hand was farther back, so the snake crawled past and paid no attention to it. Fargo watched the serpent until it disappeared in some brush about ten feet away.

Then and only then did he dare to breathe again. He clenched his jaw and suppressed the shudder of revulsion and horror that went through him. Snakes didn't particularly bother him, not like they did some people, but that little striped bastard had just come *too* close, he thought.

While Fargo had been watching the snake, Linus McShane had gotten the two men his brother had told him to take with him, and now all three of them set out on foot, carrying the burlap sacks they would use to bring back supplies. Still curious as to their destination, Fargo wriggled backward, away from the camp, until he thought it was safe to stand up again. As he listened, he heard Linus and the other two men moving through the woods.

Fargo decided to trail them. Someone in the area had to be working with the river pirates, and he wanted to find out who it was. He already suspected Jonas Baxter, but it would be nice to have confirmation.

The men moved fairly quickly, which told Fargo they were following a trail of some sort. He didn't have that luxury. He had to make his own path through the woods, and he had to be quiet about it, too. He couldn't just go thrashing through the brush, or Linus and the other two men might hear him and realize they were being followed.

A grim smile touched Fargo's mouth as he made his way through the forest. He was known for being able to find his way where other men couldn't. That was how he had come to be called the Trailsman. But in these piney woods even he might get lost and wander around aimlessly. He already wasn't sure how to get back to the spot where he had left the Ovaro.

That would be a particularly ignominious end, he thought, tramping around out here until a gator or a snake got him. He was determined not to let that happen.

Linus and the others got ahead of him, and he began having trouble hearing them. Fargo was about to start moving faster, even though it was a risk, when he heard some other noises. They continued, and after a few seconds, he recognized them as the sound of ax blades biting deep into the trunks of trees.

He paused and thought about that, finding it very interesting. A crew of loggers had to be working somewhere nearby. Was that where Linus McShane and the other two men were headed?

There was one good way to find out. Fargo followed the sound of the axes.

A few minutes later, he came to another cleared area. This one wasn't natural, either, and was dotted with stumps like the one where the river pirates' camp was located. Drag marks showed where mule teams had been hitched up to the felled trees with chains so the trees could be hauled away. This was the skid road, where the trees were taken out of the forest.

The loggers were working to Fargo's right, far enough away that he couldn't see them. Staying in the cover of trees that hadn't been cut down yet, he moved in that direction.

He couldn't hear Linus McShane and the other men anymore. The *thunk!* of the ax blades and the shouts of the loggers as they worked drowned out any other sounds. Fargo proceeded with great care, and a minute later he came in sight of the crew.

They were all big, powerful men with broad shoulders and heavily muscled arms, made that way by swinging an ax hour after hour, day after day, week after week. They wore overalls, flannel or homespun shirts, shapeless hats, and work boots with metal calks on the soles to give them better purchase. Some had climbed high in the pines, "topping" the trees or cutting off the upper section where most of the branches were. Others used axes or long, crosscut handsaws to cut through the base and do the actual felling. On a few occasions in the past, Fargo had found himself temporarily working as a logger, so he knew how the various jobs were done.

From the concealment of the trees, he studied the men, looking for familiar faces. He didn't spot Nick Dirkson or any of the other men who had jumped him in Jefferson the day before, so he didn't know if this crew worked for Jonas Baxter or Lawrence Kiley or maybe even one of the smaller timber outfits. Nor did he see Linus McShane or Linus's two companions, Wilcox and Patton.

Fargo watched the loggers for a few minutes and

had begun to think that maybe he'd made a mistake by assuming that the river pirates were coming here. Then he heard a distinctive bird call, the cry of the bobwhite, and knew he had been right after all. The bird call was a good one, almost indistinguishable from the real thing, but Fargo knew it had been made by a man.

That had to be a signal of some sort, and sure enough, after a few more minutes one of the loggers pulled a bright red bandanna from his pocket, took off his hat and mopped sweat off his forehead, and then walked off into the trees after leaning his ax against a stump. He could have been going off to relieve himself, but Fargo believed it was more than that.

He slipped through the woods, angling in the same general direction as the logger. Calling on all the stealth at his command, he closed in on the man, who wasn't taking any great pains to be quiet as he tramped through the woods.

The man stopped, and Fargo heard the low mutter of voices. One of them sounded like the rumbling tones of Linus McShane. A moment later, as Fargo crouched and carefully moved some brush aside, he spotted the logger, who was engaged in quiet, earnest conversation with Linus and the other two river pirates.

"—nobody in camp right now," the logger was saying. "You can slip in and raid the cookshack without anybody bein' the wiser."

"The cook'll know when he gets back from Jefferson," Linus pointed out.

"Yeah, but he'll blame the men. They're always tryin' to sneak food. He'll think that some of 'em came back in and stole the supplies while he was gone."

Linus nodded. "All right, if you're sure. This better not be a trick, though. If we get caught, Mike'll have your hide."

"I've cooperated just fine so far, haven't I?" the logger snapped. "I've tipped you boys off about the shipments down the bayou, so you'll know which ones to hit and which ones to leave alone. Your brother's been glad to get my help so far."

"Yeah, but don't push your luck," Linus said with a scowl. "If you'll double-cross one fella, you'll double-cross another, I always say."

"Don't you worry about that. The share I'm getting is enough to make sure I don't double-cross you and Red Mike."

Linus nodded. He raised a hand in farewell, then he and his companions turned and slipped off through the woods. Fargo watched the logger for a moment longer. He still didn't know which of the timber operations the man worked for, but clearly he was in league with the river pirates.

Instead of following Linus and the other two, Fargo backed away and tried to orient himself. He looked around, tipping his head back so that he could search through the canopy of boughs for the sun. He knew that by now the afternoon had to be well advanced, so when he caught a glimpse of the sun through the trees, he knew which direction was west. That knowledge allowed him to cut across country toward the spot where he had left the Ovaro, instead of being forced to retrace the convoluted path that had brought him here.

Once he was well away from the loggers and the pirates, he climbed part of the way up a tree to double-check his location. Satisfied that he was heading in the right direction, he shinnied back down and started off again.

Fargo's instincts proved to be trustworthy, as usual. He reached a stream he recognized as Alligator Slough. From there it was a simple matter to turn south, follow the stream, and get back to Big Cypress Bayou. The stallion might have wandered a little, but he would be somewhere close by the spot where the slough ran into the bayou.

Fargo started in that direction, but he hadn't gone very far before he heard voices coming toward him. Not wanting to run into anybody without knowing who it was first, he ducked deeper into the trees and crouched behind a thick-trunked pine to wait.

Several roughly dressed men came in sight. They carried axes, and one of the men used his to mark blazes on some of the trees. Another commented, "There's some good growth here. Mr. Kiley did a fine job gettin' a lease to cut this area."

So they were some of Kiley's men, Fargo thought, scouting out timber for Kiley's crews to harvest. The crew he had seen earlier was about two miles from here, so he suspected that they were working for Jonas Baxter.

Fargo was thinking about stepping out and introducing himself to Kiley's men, but before he could make up his mind whether to do that, several shots smashed through the humid air. One of the loggers let out a howl of pain, dropped his ax, and clapped his hands to his right thigh, where blood had suddenly appeared on his overalls.

His companions grabbed his arms and hustled him toward the slough as more shots blasted and bullets whistled around their heads. The three men dived into the cover of a tangle of cypress roots at the edge of the water.

Fargo didn't know who the bushwhackers were, but since the men who'd been ambushed worked for Kiley, it stood to reason that the ones trying to kill them were some of Baxter's men. He couldn't see the gunmen, but he could hear where the shots were coming from. Drawing his Colt, he began working his way in that direction.

The time that it took Fargo to close in on the bushwhackers must have seemed a lot longer to the men who were hunkered among the roots at the edge of the slough, trying to stay low enough that they wouldn't get killed. Fargo came up behind the four men who were firing from the shelter of some pines. They were dressed like loggers, too, but right then they were working at the business of murder.

The men were spread out, with ten or fifteen yards between each of them. Fargo moved up behind the closest one, reversed his Colt, and brought the heavy revolver's butt crashing down on the man's head. Without even a groan, the man dropped his rifle, fell to his knees, and toppled over onto his face, out cold.

Fargo darted back, hoping the attack hadn't been noticed by the others. They were so busy trying to kill Kiley's men that that seemed to be the case. Fargo cat-footed toward the second man. He knew he couldn't knock all of them out of the fight without alerting the others, but he wanted to cut down the odds as much as he could.

Before he could strike again, though, somebody yelled, "Hey!" and he twisted around to see a big bruiser he recognized as Nick Dirkson. Dirkson was carrying an ax, and with a snarl of hate, he threw it at Fargo.

Loggers practiced such moves; they even had ax-throwing competitions in their leisure time. So the double-bitted ax flew through the air at the Trailsman with deadly speed and accuracy. If not for Fargo's own lightning-quick reflexes, the blade probably would have split his head open. As it was, he flung himself out of the way just in time. The rapidly revolving ax whirred past him.

Rifles crashed as the bushwhackers turned and spotted him. Fargo heard the wind-rip of a slug as it passed close by his ear. He dropped to one knee, brought the Colt up, and triggered twice. As the revolver bucked against his palm, he saw one of the gunmen spin off his feet, driven down by a bullet.

But the odds were still against Fargo, and Dirkson had pulled a gun from a pocket in his overalls and started shooting, too. Chunks of pine bark flew from the trunk of a tree as Fargo threw himself behind it. He heard the bullets thudding into the trunk.

"Spread out some more!" Dirkson called to his men. "We'll get him in a cross fire!"

"What about those other fellas?" asked one of the bushwhackers.

"Forget about them! I want Fargo!"

Fargo didn't recall telling Dirkson his name the day before. The man must have asked around about him and found out who he was. Dirkson might even know that Fargo had had breakfast with Lawrence Kiley that morning, which would make him more convinced than ever that Fargo was an enemy.

Things had certainly gone too far to head off trouble by talking. Fargo pressed his back against the tree trunk as he reloaded the chambers in the Colt's cylinder that he had emptied. He wished he had his Henry rifle, but it was still in its sheath on the Ovaro's saddle.

He couldn't wait for Dirkson and the others to close in on him. If he did, they would have him right where they wanted him. It would be better to take the fight to them, and that suited Fargo's nature more anyway. He took a deep breath and then darted toward another tree.

"Watch it!" Dirkson yelled as a gun roared. "He's moving!"

Fargo twisted as he ran and snapped a shot toward the muzzle flash he had seen from the corner of his eye. A sharp cry told him his shot had either scored or else come mighty close. He dived behind a clump of brambles as bullets whistled above him.

The brush hid him but wouldn't stop a slug, so he knew he couldn't stay there. He crawled a couple of yards, then leaped up and doubled back. One of the bushwhackers came around a tree right in front of him, obviously startled. The man hadn't expected to run into Fargo this way. He tried to bring his rifle up.

Fargo struck first, lashing out with his left fist. The punch landed with stunning impact on the man's jaw and staggered him. Fargo laid the barrel of the Colt against the side of his head. Even though the blow was blunted somewhat by the hat the man wore, the solid thud as it landed told Fargo the man wasn't going to have any fight left in him. Sure enough, the man's eyes rolled up in their sockets, and he collapsed in a limp sprawl.

That brought the odds down to two to one. Fargo leaped over the body of the man he had just knocked out and headed for the slough. He hoped Kiley's men had taken advantage of the opportunity to get the hell out of there.

Fargo emerged from the pines and saw that the three loggers were gone. Obviously, the one who had been hit wasn't wounded so badly that he couldn't travel with the help of the other two. Fargo was glad they had gotten away. He wanted them to be able to testify that some of Jonas Baxter's men had ambushed them.

Before Fargo could figure out what to do next, Dirkson burst out of the brush beside him with a furious roar like that of a maddened black bear. Dirkson was almost as big as a bear, and Fargo didn't have time to brace himself before the man crashed into him. He and Dirkson both toppled off the bank, falling into the slough among the cypress roots.

Fargo still had hold of his gun. He slashed at Dirkson's head with it as they grappled, throwing up huge splashes of the murky, shallow water. Dirkson grabbed the wrist of Fargo's gun hand. The fingers clamped shut like iron bands around Fargo's wrist. Fargo got his other hand on Dirkson's muscular throat and hung on for dear life as they continued to wrestle, rolling over and over in the stream. Fargo tried to hold Dirkson's head under the surface, not really trying to drown him, just hoping that maybe being forced to swallow some of the foul stuff would make Dirkson stop fighting.

Dirkson continued to thrash, though, and a wild blow that he swung clipped Fargo on the side of the head. Half stunned, Fargo lost his grip on his enemy. With a triumphant yell, Dirkson tore free and smashed a malletlike fist against Fargo's chest. Fargo sprawled backward in the water.

Dirkson loomed above him and reached behind his belt to pull out a hatchet, a tool that loggers sometimes used to trim smaller branches from felled trees. As he lifted it, his face contorted in an evil grin. Since he was soaked from the slough and had moss and slime dripping from his hair, it was a truly hideous expression as he threatened, "I'm gonna chop you in little pieces, Fargo."

It was what Fargo saw when he glanced past Dirkson that made his blood run cold, though.

Three sets of reptilian eyes were visible above the surface of the slough, followed by the scaly humps of long, swiftly moving bodies as a trio of alligators arrowed through the water straight toward Fargo and Dirkson.

7

After being immersed in the murky water of the slough, Fargo's Colt probably wasn't going to work again until he had cleaned and dried it thoroughly, so he couldn't blast one of the alligators and hope that the other two would go for the wounded beast instead of him and Dirkson.

So he called out, "Behind you, Dirkson! Gators!"

Dirkson's grin widened as he said, "You don't think I'm gonna fall for that old trick, do you, Fargo?"

Fargo didn't really care whether Dirkson believed him or not. He didn't want to be dragged under the water, drowned, and left to rot in some gator's lair until he was a tasty morsel for the scaly varmints.

Instead he rolled over, turning his back on Dirkson. Then he surged to his feet and headed for solid ground as fast as he could move. Water splashed high around him.

Fargo's action seemed to take Dirkson by surprise, judging by the baffled look that replaced the grin on his face. He twisted around, saw the alligators only a few feet away in the slough, and let out a bloodcurdling screech.

The bank wasn't that far away, so Fargo was able to reach it in a couple of bounds. When he did, he looked back to see Dirkson going the other way, toward the far side of the slough with the alligators right behind him. Fargo didn't have any liking for the man, but neither did he want to see Dirkson gobbled up by gators. He looked around, spotted a broken cypress branch lying on the ground nearby, snatched it up, and flung it as hard as he could at the alligator closest to Dirkson.

Fargo's aim was good. The branch slammed against the gator's snout, taking it by surprise and making it jerk around and thrash in the water as it searched for whatever had hit it. That distracted the other gators, too, and gave Dirkson time to launch himself out of the water in a frantic dive toward the bank. He landed on the ground and rolled to put even more distance between himself and the alligators. The beasts would sometimes leave the water and pursue prey on solid ground, and they were fast there, too.

Dirkson was already running when he came to his feet. He dashed into the woods, vanishing from Fargo's sight. Fargo figured Dirkson had forgotten all about wanting to kill him. Nearly getting eaten by alligators had scared that desire right out of him.

The other bushwhackers were around somewhere, and the threat from them, as well as the gators, convinced Fargo not to linger in the vicinity. He pulled back into the woods, far enough so that the alligators would be unlikely to come after him, but still close enough he could see the slough and follow it back to Big Cypress Bayou.

Fargo moved fast, trotting through the pines and keeping an eye out for more trouble. Nothing else happened, though, and about a quarter of an hour later he came out on the bank of the bayou. The Ovaro stood there cropping at grass. The big stallion threw his head up and nickered a greeting as Fargo appeared.

"Told you I'd be back," Fargo said to the horse

with a smile. He hadn't really been gone all that long, he realized as he looked up at the sun, maybe a couple of hours. But a lot had happened during that time.

He had found the camp of the river pirates, discovered a definite link between McShane's gang and Jonas Baxter, and prevented Nick Dirkson and the other bushwhackers from murdering three of Lawrence Kiley's men. Any way you looked at it, that was a good day's work.

But the day wasn't over yet, Fargo told himself as he swung up into the saddle and headed back toward Jefferson.

By the time he reached the settlement, he realized that something he had seen or heard today didn't seem right. But his sojourn in the piney woods had been so hectic that he couldn't put his finger on whatever it was that was bothering him.

His buckskins had dried after his dunking in the slough. He left the Ovaro at the stable and walked toward the Excelsior House, thinking he might change clothes anyway. Along the way, however, he passed a building with KILEY TIMBER COMPANY lettered in gilt on the front window. Fresh buckskins could wait. He went inside and found Lawrence Kiley working behind a desk with a lot of papers and ledgers spread out in front of him.

"I'm surprised you don't have a clerk to handle all those chores," Fargo said with a smile.

"I do, but he's sick," Kiley replied. "Came down with the blasted swamp fever. Anyway, I'm trying to figure out what to do about my shipping problems, so this needs my attention." A hopeful look lit up his round face. "You don't have any good news to report about that, do you, Mr. Fargo?"

"Well, I don't know." Fargo perched a hip on a corner of the desk. "I found McShane's hideout. Captain Russell told me the *Bayou Princess* was attacked not long after she passed Alligator Slough, so I rode up there and had a look around."

Kiley looked excited now. "And the pirates' camp was up the slough?"

"That's right," Fargo said with a nod. "About a mile north of the bayou."

"That's isolated, dangerous country out there, even though as the crow flies it's not all that far from town." Kiley thumped a fist on the desk, making some of the papers jump a little. "By God, once we tell Sheriff Higgins about this, he'll *have* to do something!"

"There's more," Fargo said. "Did you have some men scouting for good timber to cut out in that area today, say a half mile or so west of the slough?"

Kiley nodded. "I recently signed a lease out there, so I sent three men in that direction to check it out, but I don't know how far they got. They haven't reported back in yet."

"One of them has been shot," Fargo said. He knew that was breaking the news in a pretty blunt fashion, and Kiley looked shocked. "I don't think he was hurt too bad. He and the two men with him got away from the varmints who bushwhacked them."

"You saw this yourself?"

"I pitched in to give them a hand. The bushwhackers got away, though."

"Did you see who they were?" Kiley asked, his expression a mixture of anger and eagerness.

"One of them was Nick Dirkson," Fargo said. "I didn't know the other men, but I reckon they were some of Baxter's men, too."

Kiley slammed his fist down on the desk again. "I knew it! I just knew it! That bastard is behind everything!" He came to his feet. "I'm going to go have it out with him right now!"

Fargo straightened from his casual pose. "Are you sure that's a good idea?"

"Now that we have proof, why not? I'm going to get Sheriff Higgins and demand that he arrest Baxter!"

Kiley grabbed his beaver hat from a hook and started toward the door. Fargo went with him, thinking that maybe Kiley was right. It might be time to bring everything out in the open.

Kiley marched straight down the street to a sturdy, timber-and-stone building that housed the sheriff's office and the jail. He threw the door open, stomped in, and roared, "Higgins! Where are you?"

A bulky middle-aged man with salt-and-pepper hair and a drooping mustache came into the room through a door that probably led into the cell block. He glared at Kiley and asked with obvious dislike, "What do you want?"

"Three of my men have been attacked, and Jonas Baxter was responsible for it!"

Sheriff Higgins frowned. "That's a mighty serious charge," he said. "You got any proof?"

Kiley threw out an arm and pointed dramatically at Fargo, who had come into the office behind him. "Mr. Fargo saw the whole thing!"

Higgins looked at Fargo with narrowed eyes. "Fargo, eh? I heard you were in town. Heard a lot of stories about you, too, but I never believed 'em. Sounded like a bunch of bull to me."

"Well, you can believe this," Fargo said. "I saw Dirkson and a few other gents ambush those men who were working for Mr. Kiley. Dirkson did his damnedest to kill me, too."

Acting unconcerned, Higgins sauntered over to a cast-iron stove on which a coffeepot was staying warm. He poured himself a cup, blew on the hot liquid, and took a deliberate sip before saying, "Is that so? What happened to the fellas who allegedly got bushwhacked?"

"One of them caught a slug in the leg, but he was able to get away with the help of the others."

"Where are they now?"

Kiley said, "We don't know. They haven't gotten back yet."

"And the bushwhackers?" Higgins asked as he looked at Fargo. "You catch any of them?"

"They got away," Fargo replied.

Higgins took another sip of coffee. "So what it amounts to is I got nothin' to go on but your word, Fargo. For all I know, none of these things you're talkin' about ever even happened."

Fargo's voice was hard as flint as he replied, "You've got my word. That's enough."

"Not for the law," Higgins said.

Kiley let out a bitter curse. "I should've known better than to think you'd do your job, Higgins. You're so deep in Baxter's pocket you may never see daylight again!"

The coffee cup clattered as Higgins set it on the stove. "Hey, now!" he said as his face darkened in anger. "You can't talk to me that way! I'm the law in this county."

"Then act like it, damn it!"

"I *am* acting like it. I want real proof before I go accusin' a prominent citizen of any wrongdoing."

Kiley turned away in disgust and said to Fargo, "Come on. We're wasting our time here."

"What are you gonna do?" Higgins demanded.

"That's none of your business," Kiley said over his shoulder.

"It damned sure is! If you try to take the law into your own hands, Kiley, you'll be sorry. And if I hear anything about you harassing Mr. Baxter, I'll lock you up. I swear I will!"

Kiley ignored the sheriff and stomped out of the office without looking back. Fargo lingered for a moment, saying to Higgins, "When those men who were bushwhacked by Dirkson come in, you'll see that I was telling the truth."

67

"Bring 'em here when they do," Higgins said. "I'll be glad to listen to their story."

Fargo gave the lawman a curt nod and followed Kiley out of the office. Kiley had paused in the street to mutter darkly to himself. He turned to Fargo and said, "I'm going to talk to Baxter."

"Are you sure that's a good idea, as upset as you are right now?"

"I won't be any less upset later. When Baxter resorts to attempted murder, he's gone too damned far!"

Fargo felt pretty much the same way, so he nodded and said, "I'll come with you." After hearing so much about Jonas Baxter the past couple of days—and none of it good—he wanted to get a look at the man for himself.

Kiley led the way down Austin Street and turned the corner onto Polk. "I've been staying at the Excelsior House," he explained to Fargo as they headed for the edge of town, "but Baxter rented himself a house."

It was more than a house, Fargo saw a couple of minutes later as they came up to the place. It was a mansion, a three-story heap with lots of gables and cornices. Set against the backdrop of the thick piney woods the way it was, the house had a distinctly sinister air about it. Fargo wondered wryly if anybody named Usher or Pyncheon had ever lived there. The mansion looked like it could have come right out of a story by Poe or Hawthorne.

Kiley opened a gate in the fence around the house and marched up the walk to the porch. He crashed the heavy brass knocker against the door several times. The way the place looked, Fargo halfway expected some cadaverous gent in butler's livery to answer the summons.

Instead, when the door swung open one of the prettiest women he had seen in a while stood there, a smile on her face. Thick auburn curls spilled around

68

her shoulders, and green eyes took in the visitors. She had a slight dimple in her chin and well-formed cheekbones. A long-sleeved, high-necked, bottle-green dress was tight enough to show off the trim waist and the ample curves of her breasts. Something about her immediately struck Fargo as familiar, as if he had seen her somewhere before, even though he knew the likelihood of that was slim.

"Mr. Kiley," she said, and even though she was smiling, her voice was cool, "what can I do for you?" Her gaze moved to Fargo, and he saw appreciation flare in her eyes as she looked him over. "And who is this?"

"Mr. Fargo, an associate of mine," Kiley said as he and Fargo both took their hats off. "I need to talk to your husband."

"Won't you come in, then?" the woman asked as she moved back, still holding the door. Fargo and Kiley accepted the invitation and stepped into a foyer with a fancy hardwood floor and several gloomy paintings on the walls.

"Jonas is in the library," she went on as she closed the door. "I'll take you to him."

As the two men followed her along a hallway, Fargo admired the sway of her hips. It seemed to be a natural motion, not something that was calculated . . . although with a beautiful woman, you could never tell what was calculated and what was not.

She came to a pair of double doors and opened them. "Jonas, Lawrence Kiley and a Mr. Fargo are here to see you," she said.

An explosive grunt came from inside the room. "Kiley! What the hell does he want?"

Kiley started to bull past the woman, but something stopped him, probably ingrained chivalry. He took a deep breath, controlling his anger with a visible effort, and gave her a polite nod. "Thank you, Mrs. Baxter."

Still smiling, she held out a hand, indicating that he

and Fargo should go in. They stepped into a room made dim and shadowy by the dark wood of the walls and the leather bindings of hundreds of volumes that filled bookshelves.

A man stood behind a desk, where he had obviously just risen from a big leather chair. He had a rugged face, graying dark hair, and was tall and broad-shouldered enough that he looked like he could pick up an ax and fell a tree by himself, even now. Looking at Jonas Baxter, Fargo had a strong suspicion that the man had started out in the timber industry by doing just that.

Baxter regarded Fargo with narrowed eyes for a moment and then said, "So you're Fargo. I've heard about you."

"From Nick Dirkson?" Fargo asked.

"That's right. He told me about the fight you picked with him and some of the boys yesterday."

"Have you talked to him today?"

The question seemed to take Baxter a little by surprise. He shook his head and said, "Not since early this morning."

"Then you don't know about how he tried to kill me, after he and some other men bushwhacked three of Mr. Kiley's men and tried to kill *them*."

Another grunt escaped from Baxter. "That's a damned lie," he declared. "Kiley's always trying to stir up trouble."

"This is me telling you about it, not Mr. Kiley," Fargo pointed out.

"Then you're nothing but a troublemaker, too, Fargo, and I don't have anything to say to you."

"Then you'll have something to say to the law," Kiley said as he shook a finger at Baxter. "Competition is one thing, but you've been paying off those river pirates to disrupt my timber shipments, and now you've resorted to attempted murder!"

"That's insane! Prove it, damn you!" Baxter leaned forward, resting the knuckles of his clenched fists on the desk. His face darkened with anger.

"Now, Jonas," his wife said, "you know you shouldn't get so upset. The doctor told you it wasn't good for you."

"Not get upset?" Baxter straightened and flung a hand at Kiley. "Blast it, Francine, this ape waltzes in here and accuses me of consorting with pirates and sanctioning cold-blooded murder! I ought to thrash him and throw him out!"

Kiley took a step back and lifted his own fists. "Try it," he challenged Baxter. "Go ahead, try it."

Fargo moved so that he stood between the two men. "Settle down, both of you," he snapped.

"I haven't forgotten about you, Fargo," Baxter said. "If I was ten years younger, I'd thrash you, too! By God, I might do it anyway!"

Francine Baxter went around the desk and gripped her husband's arm. "Jonas, please sit down. I insist."

Baxter's furious glare didn't lessen any, but he allowed his wife to urge him back down into his chair. "Get out, or I'll have the sheriff on you," he told Fargo and Kiley.

"Yes, I'm well aware that Sheriff Higgins is your lapdog," Kiley said. "But I'll soon have the proof I need to put a stop to your villainy, Baxter, and if Higgins won't enforce the law, I'll find someone who will. It may be time to get a U.S. marshal in here to straighten things out!"

"Go right ahead," Baxter said with a sneer. "I've nothing to fear from the law."

The two timber barons stared at each other with hate in their eyes for a moment before Fargo touched Kiley's shoulder and said, "We're not doing any good here. Might as well move along for now, until we've talked to those fellas who got bushwhacked."

"I suppose you're right," Kiley said. He shook a finger at Baxter again. "But we'll be back. You can count on it."

"I don't count on anything except the fact that you're a lunatic," Baxter shot back.

Fargo gripped Kiley's arm and steered him out of the library. Kiley was practically apoplectic, muttering angrily to himself as he and Fargo went toward the front door of the mansion. Francine Baxter followed them. When they reached the door, she said, "Good afternoon, gentlemen. I hate to be impolite, Mr. Kiley, but I wish you wouldn't come back here. Jonas gets so upset, and it's not good for him."

Kiley just snorted, as if to ask why that should worry him, and stalked out the door, across the porch, and out the flagstone walk.

"Mr. Fargo," Francine said, quiet enough so that Kiley didn't hear. Fargo stopped on the porch and looked back at her. Her smile was more genuine now as she went on, "Perhaps you *will* come back sometime."

"So I'd be welcome?" Fargo said.

"Yes. I believe you would be."

Fargo studied her for a moment and then nodded. He went down the steps and out the walk. His long-legged strides caught up quickly with Kiley. He had to ask himself just what exactly that last exchange with Francine Baxter had meant.

Considering the bold look in her eyes, he thought he knew the answer.

"What was that about?" Kiley asked, proving that he hadn't missed the fact that Fargo lingered behind him after all.

"Nothing," Fargo said, and meant it. Francine might be interested in him, but she was a married woman. Not only that, but she was married to a fellow who was the mortal enemy of the man Fargo was working for. That made her off-limits in more ways than one.

But he had to admit that Francine Baxter was a beautiful, intriguing woman. If things had been different . . .

Then those thoughts were pushed right out of his head by the sight of Isabel Sterling standing on the porch of the Excelsior House.

8

"Hello, Skye," Isabel said as Fargo and Kiley came up to the hotel porch. "I was hoping you'd be back in time so we could have supper together."

Fargo had already begun to think about the same thing. His belly told him it was growing late and reminded him that he hadn't stopped to eat anything in the middle of the day.

"Let me clean up a mite first, and then I'd be happy to join you," he told her.

Isabel leaned closer, sniffed, and wrinkled her nose. "What *is* that smell?"

Fargo grinned. "I went for a swim in Alligator Slough."

Isabel's eyes widened, and she asked, "Why in the world did you do *that*?"

Fargo nodded toward his companion. "Mr. Kiley here can tell you all about it while I'm washing up and changing clothes."

"I'd be glad to," Kiley said. "Let's go inside, my dear."

Kiley was still angry at Baxter, but he had recovered his usual charm and politeness. He linked arms with Isabel and they went into the lobby to sit down in armchairs flanking one of the potted plants. Fargo crossed to the stairs, ignoring the supercilious expression on the face of the desk clerk, and went up to his room.

As he washed up and pulled on his last set of clean buckskins, he hoped that he wouldn't be rolling around in a slimy, gator-infested slough again anytime soon. By the time he got downstairs and rejoined Isabel and Kiley, Isabel had a worried look on her face. Fargo knew Kiley had filled her in on the day's events.

"Skye, you nearly got killed!" she said as she stood up and grasped his hands.

"Nearly doesn't count," Fargo said with a smile. "I'm fine." He turned to Kiley. "You want to join us for dinner?"

Kiley shook his head. "No, I'm going to go look for those three men who were ambushed. They should have been back by now. You said one of them was wounded, so they might be down at Doc Fearn's place."

After Kiley left the hotel, Fargo and Isabel walked into the dining room and sat down at one of the empty tables. After the waitress had brought coffee and they had ordered their meals, Isabel reached across the table to grasp one of Fargo's hands again and said, "I hate to think about you out there putting your life in danger, Skye."

"Folks put their lives in danger every time they get out of bed in the morning," Fargo pointed out. "There's no guarantee that anybody will live to see the sun set."

"No, but some people go out of their way to take chances." She sighed. "I know you're just trying to help Mr. Kiley, and Captain Russell, too. I'm grateful for that, because Cap'n Andy has been almost like a father to me for the past year, ever since . . ."

Fargo frowned as her voice trailed off. "Ever since what, if you don't mind my asking?"

Isabel shook her head. Obviously, she did mind.

"It's nothing important," she said. "I had some trouble, and Captain Russell was there to help me. That's all. I feel like I'm in his debt, though, and I'll do anything I can to help him in return."

"That's a good attitude to have," Fargo said. He didn't press Isabel for answers about her past. That was her business, unless she chose to make it otherwise.

When the food came, it was good, and Fargo ate with a hearty appetite, replenishing his strength after the long day. As they lingered over coffee, he smiled across the table at Isabel and asked, "Do you have any plans for the evening?"

"As a matter of fact, I do," she said. Before Fargo's smile could widen into a grin, she went on. "I'd like to hunt up a good poker game." She flexed her long, slender fingers. "I need to stay in practice."

Fargo chuckled. Although he'd had something else in mind when he asked the question, the thought of a few hands of cards sounded pretty good to him, too. And he found himself curious as to what sort of poker player Isabel was. There was one good way to find out.

"I'll join you, if that's all right."

She returned his smile. "I was hoping you would."

As they left the dining room and entered the lobby, Fargo inclined his head toward the clerk and said in a low voice, "Should I ask him where we can find a game?"

"And have him make that face like a prune again?" Isabel shook her head. "Don't worry, Skye. I've been traveling on the *Bayou Princess* for a while now, and staying over on these stops in Jefferson. I know where to find a good game."

That turned out to be a saloon called Skinner's, which was located in a brick building on Lafayette Street. The main room looked more like somebody's parlor than a barroom, with polished hardwood floors, nice rugs, and crystal chandeliers. Felt-covered gaming tables took up some of the space. Instead of booths, there were more tables and armchairs. A long mahogany bar with a well-stocked back bar and a large gilt-framed mirror behind it were the only saloonlike touches. The hostesses wore long, rather demure dresses instead of gaudy, spangled outfits, and the bartenders sported nice jackets, vests, and bow ties. Most of the customers were well-dressed, soft-spoken men.

Fargo looked around and said to Isabel, "You sure we didn't fall in a hole somewhere and come out in Philadelphia or Boston?"

"You wouldn't expect to find a place like this in the piney woods of East Texas, would you?" she asked with a smile.

"Not hardly."

"Between the cotton and timber industries, Jefferson is a wealthy town, Skye. It's almost like a much smaller version of New Orleans."

The way she spoke about that Louisiana city made Fargo think that she knew it well, and he wondered if that was where she was from. He wondered, too, if that was where the incident occurred that had caused Isabel to seek help from Captain Andy Russell.

He didn't ask, though, still willing to give Isabel her privacy. Instead he went with her to one of the tables where a poker game was in progress. Four men were playing in a rather desultory manner, but they perked up when Isabel arrived. That would be a natural reaction for most men, but evidently these gents were acquainted with her.

"Good to see you again, Miss Sterling," one of them greeted her. "Would you care to join the game once this hand is over?"

"I would," Isabel said, "and so would my friend here."

The man who had spoken extended a hand to Fargo. "Edgar Price," he introduced himself. "I own a cotton plantation west of here."

Fargo shook hands and supplied his name.

"I'd heard you were in town, Mr. Fargo," Price said. "These other gentlemen are Hal Olmsted, Howard Phillips, and Patrick Walser."

Fargo greeted the others, who all had the look of confident, successful businessmen. He held one of the empty chairs for Isabel and then sat down himself as the men concluded the hand they were playing, with big, bluff Patrick Walser winning the pot. Everyone threw in their antes again, including Fargo and Isabel this time.

Out of habit, Fargo was sitting where he could keep an eye on the door. That was why he saw the man with the eye patch come in. Fargo recognized him right away as the man he had thought might be following him the day before. This time, though, the man didn't even glance in Fargo's direction with his one good eye. He just went straight to the bar and ordered a drink.

In his rough clothes, he was a little out of place in Skinner's, but no more so than Fargo in his buckskins. Nor were they the only patrons who weren't wearing suits. There were a few others. Evidently anyone was welcome in the place as long as he behaved himself and had money to pay for the drinks he ordered.

Despite the fact that the one-eyed man had ignored him, Fargo watched the hombre from the corner of his own eye. That didn't interfere with his poker playing. He was still able to keep his mind on the game.

That was fortunate, because Isabel and the four men from Jefferson proved to be good players. They weren't afraid to take a chance when they thought their cards justified it, but neither were they reckless, foolish plungers. They were just the sort of canny opponents who could give Fargo a good game. And Isabel was perhaps the shrewdest one of all, with an almost infallible instinct for when to push her luck. Fargo might have thought that she was cheating, if not

78

for the fact that his keen eyes watched her with close scrutiny. He was able to spot any trick that a card-sharp might try, and Isabel indulged in none of them.

Convivial talk flowed freely around the table. Fargo enjoyed himself a great deal and wasn't really aware of how much time was passing, although he did notice when the one-eyed man left the saloon after a couple of drinks, still without paying any attention to the Trails-man. Fargo was down a few dollars, as were the other male players, which made Isabel the big winner. None of the men appeared to mind, though, proof of Fargo's theory that most men were more willing to lose at poker to a beautiful woman than they were to another man.

Finally, at the end of a hand when Isabel raked in another sizable pot, she smiled and said, "I believe that will do it for me, gentlemen."

There were halfhearted protests from Price, Olmsted, Phillips, and Walser, and entreaties for her to give them another chance to win some of their money back, but Isabel shook her head.

"A girl has to get her beauty sleep, you know," she said.

"My dear, you appear to have gotten plenty," Price said. He sighed. "But of course we'll be gracious and let you go, won't we, boys?"

A chorus of agreement came from the other players.

Isabel gathered her winnings and tucked them into her handbag. Fargo held her chair for her as she got up, and the other men stood politely. She looked around at them, nodded, and said, "Gentlemen." Then she offered her arm to Fargo, who took it and strolled toward the door with her.

He had seen the looks of jealousy in the eyes of the other men. Those hombres had something to be jealous about, he thought, and it didn't have anything to do with the money they'd lost tonight. He was leaving with Isabel, and they weren't.

So to Fargo's way of thinking, that sort of made *him* the big winner of the evening. . . .

She came into his arms almost as soon as the door of her room in the hotel closed behind them, and their kiss and the way they tugged at each other's clothes demonstrated the urgency of passion postponed until now. Fargo slid his tongue between Isabel's eager lips as they parted. He filled his hands with the firm bounty of her breasts as her dress fell around her waist.

As they left Skinner's a few minutes earlier, he had looked around for the man with the eye patch, just in case that hombre was lurking in the vicinity of the saloon, but Fargo hadn't seen any sign of him. Nor had they run into any other trouble on their walk back to the Excelsior House.

Now all of Fargo's senses were concentrated on the warm, willing woman in his arms. They stripped each other's clothes off, their arousal growing hotter with each new area of skin that was revealed. The night was warm, the sort of sultry evening made for passion.

When they were both nude, Fargo pulled Isabel tightly against him, cupped a hand behind her head, and kissed her again. She slid a hand down between them to caress the long, thick pole of his manhood as it prodded its heated length against her belly. She urged Fargo back until they reached the bed. Then he sprawled on the mattress while she positioned herself beside his hips. Wrapping both hands around his shaft, she leaned over and began to kiss and lick the head.

Fargo closed his eyes and lay there for long moments, basking in the sheer pleasure of what she was doing to him. He felt the heat of her mouth engulf him as she sucked in as much of his organ as she could. One hand steadied him while the other crept down between his legs to cup the heavy sacs at the base of his shaft.

A part of Fargo's mind would have been content to just lie there and let her bring him to culmination this way, but at the same time that seemed a mite selfish to him. So he opened his eyes and reached out to grasp her hips. She answered his gentle tugs by moving around so that she was above him, with her thighs straddling his head while her upper body rested on his stomach. She never stopped sucking, even while she was rearranging herself.

With her poised like that, Fargo was able to reach up and use his thumbs to spread apart the folds of her sex. He sent his tongue delving into it. That made a shudder go through her, and she finally stopped what she was doing to lift her head from his groin and gasp in ecstasy. Then she went right back to her task with renewed energy.

Both of them continued their oral caresses for long minutes, each selflessly giving the other pleasure. Finally, when they couldn't stand the exquisite torment any longer, Isabel rolled off of Fargo onto her back and spread her legs. He knelt between her thighs, brought the head of his member to her drenched opening, and drove into her. She was so wet and he was so hard that he was able to sheathe himself fully within her with one thrust.

Isabel wrapped her arms and legs around him and pushed her tongue into his mouth as they kissed. Fargo launched into the timeless, universal rhythm of men and women coupling. The only sounds in the room were their labored breathing and the soft, liquid music of their joining.

Despite the long, action-packed day, Fargo's desire allowed him to find fresh reserves of strength. He was tireless in his lovemaking, and his pounding thrusts soon sent Isabel spiraling over the edge into a climax. He eased off a bit as she clutched at him and spasmed around him. When the shudders rippling through her trailed away, he allowed her to catch her breath for a moment, then resumed his urgent pace. She looked up at him in amazement and whispered, "Skye, you didn't . . . ?"

Fargo smiled and kept going.

Isabel gasped as she felt her arousal building back up. Fargo was relentless, and when she climaxed again he had to kiss her to keep her from screaming in pleasure. This time Fargo let himself go as well, relaxing the iron control that he had exercised earlier. He drove his shaft into her as far as it would go and began to empty himself in spurt after shuddering spurt. His juices filled her to overflowing. Their shared culmination left both of them limp and drenched and covered with a fine sheen of sweat.

With his manhood still inside her, Fargo tightened his arms around her and rolled onto his back, so that she wound up sprawled atop him. He felt the fast, steady thudding of her heart against his chest. His right hand stroked her fair hair as she rested her head on his shoulder, while his left caressed the swelling curve of her rump.

Isabel was too breathless to speak for several minutes. When she finally recovered enough to find her voice again, she lifted her head and said, "Skye, even . . . even after last night . . . I didn't know it could be so good."

Fargo chuckled. "Practice makes most things better, or so they say."

She laughed, too, and said, "In that case, I intend to get a lot of practice with you."

She pushed herself up a little, leaned over, and blew out the bedside lamp, plunging the room into darkness. Fargo didn't know what she had in mind to do next, but he was pretty sure he would enjoy it, whatever it was.

Unfortunately, he didn't get the chance to, because at that moment he glanced over Isabel's shoulder toward the window. The curtain was pulled, but it was thin enough so that some of the moonlight from outside came through it.

And that silvery illumination was enough for him to be able to make out the silhouette of a man crouched on the balcony just outside the window.

Somebody was spying on them.

9

Fargo clamped his arms around Isabel and moved again, this time rolling right off the bed. He twisted so that he landed on the bottom as they fell to the floor. Isabel cried out, not in pleasure this time but from surprise.

Eavesdropping on their lovemaking was bad enough, but the lurker on the balcony might have something even worse in mind. Fargo wouldn't have been surprised if the glass in the window had shattered under the onslaught of bullets. The man might have come to ambush them, not just spy on them.

No shots came, though, and as Fargo pushed Isabel off of him, she said in alarm, "Skye, what—"

"Stay down," Fargo told her as he snagged his Colt from the holster he had placed on a chair beside the bed. He saw that the shadow of the lurker had disappeared from the curtain. The faint sound of running footsteps came to his ears.

The son of a bitch was getting away.

Naked as a jaybird, Fargo leaped up and lunged to the window. He swept the curtain aside with his left hand and thrust the window up. He went through the opening in a low dive that sent him sprawling on the balcony. Given the fact that he was naked, that was a mite painful, but he didn't care at the moment. He spotted a shape in the darkness several yards away and identified it as a man trying to climb over the wrought-iron railing at the front of the balcony.

"Hold it!" Fargo called as he lifted the Colt.

Halfway over the railing, the spy twisted around. Colt flame bloomed in the darkness as the gun in his hand erupted twice.

Fargo was already moving, rolling to the side as the slugs plowed into the planks of the balcony. He felt the sting of splinters in bare flesh, but that was better than the smash of bullets. As he came to rest on his stomach again he triggered the Colt and felt it buck against his hand as fire gouted from the muzzle. The flash lit up the balcony, and in that searing instant, he caught a glimpse of the man's face.

He wasn't a bit surprised to see the black patch over the lurker's left eye.

With a yell of pain, the man went backward over the railing, disappearing. Fargo didn't know if he'd been hit or had just lost his balance and fallen.

Fargo got to his feet and hurried over to the edge of the balcony, being careful as he peered over because he didn't want to get a faceful of lead if the one-eyed man opened fire on him from the street below. The man wasn't interested in fighting anymore, though. Instead he was running along Austin Street, limping quite a bit but moving fast despite that. Fargo snapped a shot at him, aiming low in hopes of knocking a leg out from under him, but the bullet kicked up dust in the street as the man suddenly darted sideways and vanished into the black mouth of an alley.

Fargo bit back a curse and lowered the Colt. He knew that by the time he could pull some clothes on and get downstairs, the one-eyed man would be long gone. Jefferson was a big enough town so that someone who didn't want to be found could lose himself without much trouble, even a varmint with an eye patch and an injured leg.

"Skye?" Isabel asked from the open window. Her voice was tight with worry. "Skye, are you all right?"

Fargo turned toward her and said, "Yeah, I reckon I'm fine. Skinned up a mite, that's all." He went to the window, and as Isabel stepped away from it, he threw a leg over the sill and climbed back into the darkened room.

Along the street, people had come out to see what all the shooting was about. Men yelled questions to each other, but nobody had any answers.

Fargo didn't intend to volunteer any information about his involvement in the fracas, either. He didn't want to have to try to explain things to Sheriff Higgins.

For one thing, he didn't have any real answers. He didn't know who the one-eyed man was, or why the hombre had been following him.

Or *had* the man been following him? Fargo suddenly asked himself. The bastard hadn't hesitated to start shooting, as if it didn't matter one way or the other to him whether Fargo lived or died.

If that was true, then maybe the one-eyed man had actually been spying on someone else, and Fargo just happened to have been there.

He pulled the curtain closed and then turned to Isabel, who stood near the bed. "Do you know a tall man with dark hair and an eye patch?" he asked her.

"Is . . . is that who was out there?"

"That's right," Fargo said. "I first spotted him last night, and I thought then that he was on my trail, even though I'd never seen him before. He was at Skinner's tonight and I figured the same thing. But now I'm wondering if he was actually following you."

His voice was blunt and uncompromising. He wanted answers. Being shot at always made him mighty curious.

But he wasn't prepared for the gasp of dismay that came from Isabel. As if her knees had suddenly gone weak, she clutched one of the bedposts and sat down on the mattress. "Oh, no," she said in a hushed, miserable voice. "Dear Lord, no. It can't be."

Fargo reached into the pocket of his buckskin trousers, found a lucifer, and snapped it into life with his thumbnail. He set the gun down, lifted the lamp chimney, then held the match to the wick. It caught, and as Fargo lowered the chimney, a yellow glow filled the room and showed him just how scared and distraught Isabel looked.

"What is it?" he asked. "What's wrong?"

She looked up at him with terrified eyes. Choking the words out, she said, "That man . . . that man must work for my husband. Oh, God, Skye, he's found me . . . and now he's going to kill me!"

"His name is Gideon Cutler," Isabel said a few minutes later as she sat on the edge of the bed. She had a dressing gown wrapped around her now and clutched a glass of water that Fargo had poured for her from the pitcher on the table. "I met him when I was nineteen. He was rich and powerful and handsome, and he . . . he swept me off my feet. That's the only way to put it."

Fargo had pulled on his buckskins and his boots. He buckled his gun belt around his hips as he said, "So you married him."

Isabel nodded. "Yes. I thought I wanted to spend the rest of my life with him."

Fargo thought the whole thing sounded like something out of a melodramatic novel, but he didn't say that. Anyway, real life was often stranger and more melodramatic than anything in fiction, he mused.

"I didn't know what he was really like, though," Isabel continued. "I thought that since he came from one of the finest families in New Orleans, surely he would be a gentleman."

"Having money and good breeding never kept anybody from being an evil son of a bitch if that's the way they're bent," Fargo pointed out.

"Yes, I know that now," Isabel said with a sigh. "But I was young and innocent then."

"I reckon the marriage turned out worse than you thought it would."

Another shudder went through her. She took a sip of the water and then said, "Gideon was a devil. He asked me to do things . . . terrible things . . . not just with him, but with his friends, too. They were just as bad as he was." She looked up at Fargo. "I didn't come from a wealthy family, Skye. My father was a merchant. He had to have a loan to keep his store going when business was bad. Gideon's father owned the bank." A sad smile touched her lips as she shook her head. "Gideon married me, but at heart he thought I was just a whore. So that's the way he treated me. He even told me that he owned me and that if I ever tried to leave him, he would kill me. I tried to make the best of it . . . until I couldn't stand it anymore and I . . . ran away."

"That's how you wound up on the *Bayou Princess*," Fargo guessed.

Isabel nodded. "It didn't happen right away. I left New Orleans. I had a little money I had . . . stolen . . . from Gideon." A bleak smile touched her lips. "I'd say that I earned it, but that makes me sound even more like a whore, doesn't it?"

Fargo's voice was gentle as he said, "Just go on with the story."

"Out on my own like that, I . . . I had to have some way to get along, and I didn't want to resort to selling myself. Gideon had taught me how to play poker. I found out that I was good at it, and men enjoyed playing with me. Maybe it's just another form of prostitution—"

Fargo shook his head. "Hardly."

"Anyway, I wound up in Shreveport, and that's

where I ran into Cap'n Andy. He and my father were old friends. I've known him ever since I was a little girl. When he found out what had happened, he wanted to go down to New Orleans and give Gideon a sound thrashing." Her smile held genuine warmth this time. "That's the way he put it, and he would have tried to do it, too, if I hadn't talked him out of it. I said if he would just let me travel with him on the *Bayou Princess*, that would be enough. I really didn't think Gideon would go to the trouble of hunting me down like this, especially so far away from New Orleans."

"It's not really that far," Fargo pointed out. "Just a few days by riverboat. And you said you took some money from him. Some fellas get mighty touchy about things like that."

Isabel shook her head. "It's not the money, although I'm sure that made him even angrier. It's the way I defied him. He can't stand that."

"We don't *know* that hombre with the eye patch is working for him."

"You thought he was following you, but wasn't I with you every time you saw him?"

Fargo nodded. "That's true enough."

"And he shot at you, so obviously he didn't care whether you lived or died."

"The same thought crossed my mind," Fargo said. "Everything you're saying makes sense, Isabel."

A little shudder ran through her. "Plus, I can feel it in my bones. That man has probably already sent word to Gideon that I'm here, and he's stayed in Jefferson to keep an eye on me. Gideon may already be on his way."

"Nobody's going to hurt you," Fargo said. "I'm going to see to that."

She set the glass of water aside, stood up, and put her arms around him. Fargo hugged her in return as she leaned her head against his shoulder.

"That makes me feel better, Skye," she said, "but you can't stay with me for the rest of my life. Sooner or later Gideon will catch up to me sometime when you're not around. And then . . . and then if I'm lucky he'll just kill me."

"And if you're not lucky?" Fargo said.

"He'll make me go back to New Orleans with him, and it'll start all over again."

Fargo didn't see any solution short of killing Gideon Cutler, and although some men might have been willing to commit murder for a woman like Isabel, he wasn't one of them.

But if Cutler showed up in Jefferson and tried to harm Isabel in any way or force her to go with him, all bets would be off. Fargo wouldn't hold back in that case.

"Maybe we're both wrong about this," he told her. "Maybe that gent with the eye patch was just looking to sneak into the hotel and see what he could steal."

"We both know that's not true, Skye."

"Well, I reckon we'll just have to wait and see what happens. But I can promise you this much, Isabel . . . you won't go through it alone."

She lifted her head and he kissed her again, but it wasn't passionate this time so much as it was comforting. It might have *turned* passionate if it had gone on, but at that moment Fargo heard a rapid knocking of knuckles against a door.

Not Isabel's door, though. The knocking came from across the hall, where the room he had rented was located. Somebody was looking for him.

This was a mite awkward. Fargo let go of Isabel and went to the door, held a finger to his lips to indicate she should be quiet, and opened the door a crack. Through the narrow gap he saw Lawrence Kiley standing in the hallway. Even though Fargo couldn't see Kiley's face, he got the feeling that the man was agitated about something.

As Kiley lifted his hand to knock again, Fargo opened the door of Isabel's room, stepped out into the hall, and said, "Looking for me?"

Kiley jumped a little at the sound of Fargo's voice, then turned and said, "There you are." He looked past Fargo at the door of Isabel's room and frowned.

"Somebody tried to break into Miss Sterling's room," Fargo explained. "It was during that shooting a while ago, so I figure one of the hombres involved was trying to make his getaway by ducking into her room. He didn't get in, but the whole thing scared her anyway."

"I should think so," Kiley said, apparently accepting the story, which had some elements of truth in it. Isabel had stepped into the doorway behind Fargo, with the dressing gown securely belted around her waist and the collar pulled up around her neck. "Are you all right, my dear?"

She managed to smile and nod. "I'm fine, thanks to Mr. Fargo. He heard me cry out when that awful man tried to open my window and came right across the hall to see what was wrong."

"I'd tell you that you should report this incident to the sheriff . . ." Kiley grimaced in disgust. "But Higgins is the most useless excuse for a lawman that I've ever seen. You'd be wasting your time."

"That's what I thought," Fargo said. "There was no harm done, other than Miss Sterling getting a mite spooked."

"And I'll get over that," Isabel said.

Fargo asked Kiley, "Why were you looking for me?"

Kiley sighed. "I have more bad news. Those men of mine who were bushwhacked by Dirkson this afternoon . . . ?"

Fargo nodded. Even if Kiley hadn't said that the news wasn't good, he would have had a bad feeling about this.

"They weren't at Dr. Fearn's," Kiley went on. "I couldn't find them anywhere. But a few minutes ago a man came into town driving a wagon with their bodies in the back of it. He'd found them on the trail outside of town. All three of them were dead." Kiley's voice caught a little as he added, "Shot in the back."

"Where are they now?" Fargo asked. He felt a little hollow inside. Although he had saved the men from one ambush, death had caught up to them anyway.

No, he amended to himself. *Murder* had caught up to them.

"The fellow who found them was taking them to the undertaker's. He had already reported what happened to the sheriff. Word got around quickly, spread by people who saw him coming into town with the bodies. I heard about it just a few minutes ago."

"The man who found them, is he trustworthy?" Kiley nodded. "He's an old fur trapper who's been around these parts for years, I gather. He has no connection to Baxter as far as I know. I think he probably found the men on the trail, just as he said."

Fargo nodded. "Let's go take a look." He turned back to Isabel for a moment. "You'll be all right now, Miss Sterling?"

"I'll be fine," she assured him, although Fargo saw worry still lurking in her eyes. As long as the threat of Gideon Cutler loomed over her, that worry wasn't going to go away.

But Fargo had a responsibility to Kiley, too, and it tied in with Isabel through Captain Russell, who had fallen victim to the river pirates working for Jonas Baxter. If Fargo could do something to end this war between Baxter and Kiley, then he could deal with the threat posed by Cutler without that added distraction.

His hat was still in Isabel's room, so he didn't bother to retrieve it before leaving the hotel with Kiley. Doing so would have weakened his story about going across the hall to Isabel's room because she was frightened. Fargo had the feeling that Isabel's reputation was important to her, so he would do what he could to protect it.

A crowd had gathered in front of the undertaking parlor by the time Fargo and Kiley got there. They shouldered their way through the press of curious townspeople and reached the door of the building, only to find it blocked by a tall, scrawny young man with a prominent Adam's apple and a deputy's badge pinned to his vest.

"Sheriff says can't nobody go in, Mr. Kiley," the deputy said.

"Stand aside," Kiley grated. "Those men worked for me. I have a right to see them."

The deputy looked nervous. He didn't want to go against the sheriff's orders, but the grim-faced Fargo and Kiley were pretty intimidating.

He was saved from having to make a decision when the door opened behind him and Sheriff Higgins started out of the building, only to stop short when he saw Fargo and Kiley standing there.

"You two again," Higgins grunted, clearly not pleased to see them.

"Some of my men are in there," Kiley said, nodding toward the door. "I want to see them."

Higgins thought about it for a second, then shrugged. "Come on in. I was gonna have to talk to you about this anyway, I reckon."

The three men went inside. Higgins led them through a parlor and a couple of viewing rooms to the big room in the back where the undertaker did his work. The undertaker, who was short and fat, with a shock of white hair and a surprisingly jolly smile, said, "Back already, Sheriff?" He nodded a greeting to Kiley and Fargo.

"Mr. Kiley wants to have a look at the bodies," Higgins explained.

The three dead men lay on tables with sheets pulled

over them. The undertaker nodded and went to each table in turn, drawing the sheets down so that the faces of the corpses were exposed.

Even though Fargo had seen them only briefly earlier in the day, and under hectic circumstances at that, he recognized all three of the men from the ambush. Kiley confirmed their identities by saying, "Yes, that's them. The men I sent out to scout the timber on a new lease. I guess that makes it my fault they're dead."

"The fault lies with the bastards who pulled the trigger on them," Fargo said. "You didn't have anything to do with it." He turned to the undertaker. "All three of them were shot in the back?"

"That's right," the man said, never losing his smile. "One shot apiece. Probably happened pretty fast, before they even knew what was going on."

Fargo thought that was likely, too. He suspected that Dirkson and a couple of the other bushwhackers had followed the men after Fargo disrupted the original ambush. They had caught up to the unlucky timber scouts before the men could get back to Jefferson.

Killing the men had been even more imperative after the original ambush failed, Fargo realized. Dirkson and the other killers didn't know what the three men would be able to testify to. It was possible the men would be able to identify them in court, assuming things ever got that far.

So now *he* was the only one who could tie Dirkson to the ambush, Fargo realized as he looked at the dead men.

If he hadn't had a target on his back before, he sure as hell had one painted on there now.

10

Higgins smirked as he said, "Looks like you don't have any proof that Mr. Baxter's men ambushed your boys after all, Kiley."

"I saw Dirkson and the others," Fargo said. "I can identify them."

Higgins shrugged. "It still comes down to just your word, Fargo. I've already talked to Dirkson. Two dozen men will swear that he was working with one of Mr. Baxter's crews all day, cutting timber."

"Of course they'll swear to that, you idiot!" Kiley burst out. "They work for Baxter, too."

A dark flush crept over the sheriff's face as he said, "I've taken all the abuse I'm gonna take from you, mister. One more word and I'll throw you in jail for disturbing the peace."

Kiley looked like he was ready to do more than say one more word. He looked like he was ready to take a punch at the lawman. Fargo put a hand on his shoulder and said, "Come on. There's no point in staying here."

Getting arrested wouldn't do any good. He left that thought unsaid, but Kiley seemed to get it anyway. Kiley gave a curt nod and turned away from the bodies.

"Take care of them," he said without turning around. "I want them laid to rest properly. I'll pay for it."

"Of course, Mr. Kiley," the undertaker said.

Fargo and Kiley walked out of the place. The crowd in the street was beginning to break up. Curiosity would distract people from their normal pursuits for only so long before it wore off.

"If this wasn't a war before, it is now," Kiley said in a low voice that shook slightly with anger.

"As long as Higgins is in Baxter's pocket, it's a war you won't win," Fargo pointed out. "You'd be better off lying low for a while. Tell your men to avoid Baxter's crews. In fact, they should stay as far away from where Baxter is cutting timber as possible."

"That's hard to do when so many of our leases lie right next to each other. And sometimes my men have to go through one of Baxter's leases to get to the one where they're working. Besides," Kiley added in disgust, "avoiding trouble seems too much like giving up."

"Going out of your way to find trouble isn't going to help anything," Fargo said. "There's a U.S. marshal in Shreveport. I can be back here with him in a few days, and then Higgins will have to do something."

"How are you going to get to Shreveport and back in a few days?" Kiley wanted to know.

"On the *Bayou Princess*."

Kiley stopped and looked at him. "Captain Russell's in no shape to command a riverboat again."

"He can as long as he's got a helmsman and a crew. I can handle the wheel."

Kiley rubbed his jaw and frowned in thought. "When Baxter hears about this—and it'll be impossible for you to get out of Jefferson without him hearing about it—he'll try to stop you. He'll know that he can't afford to let you come back here with a real lawman. Chances are, he'll get word to Red Mike McShane and send those river pirates after you."

"He can try that," Fargo said. "Doesn't mean he'll succeed."

"You'll be risking your life," Kiley pointed out.

"No more so than I am if I stay here and wait for Dirkson or one of Baxter's other men to bushwhack me. At least going down the bayou I'll be a moving target."

"Well, that's true, I guess," Kiley conceded. "But what about Captain Russell and the rest of the crew? They'll be in danger, too."

"No more than they have been every other trip they've made. They've already been jumped once by McShane's gang."

Kiley mulled it over some more and finally nodded. "I suppose you're right. Things have gone too far. There's no safe way out for anybody now. I'll try to keep a lid on things here while you're gone." He gave a humorless laugh. "Just don't waste any time getting back."

"We'll leave first thing in the morning," Fargo said. "I'll go talk to Captain Russell right now. He'll have to agree if we're going to do this."

Kiley laughed again, and this time it was a warmer, more genuine sound. "He's got a grudge of his own against Baxter and McShane because of the things those river rats have done in the past," Kiley said. "If I know that old gator, he'll be raring to go."

Kiley was right about Captain Russell. Sitting up in the bed in his room at Dr. Fearn's place, Russell clenched the fist on his good hand and said, "Damn right we can take the *Princess* back down the bayou. And let Red Mike and his gang do their worst. I've been itchin' for another shot at those bastards ever since I've been laid up here."

The doctor wasn't so sure that this was a good idea. "You've only had a couple of days' rest, Captain," Fearn said. "You lost a lot of blood, and you haven't recovered your strength yet."

Russell's bandaged left arm rested in a black sling.

97

"Is riding in the wheelhouse gonna hurt this wing of mine?"

Fearn shrugged and said, "Not really. Not as long as you don't do anything to break the wound open and start it bleeding again."

"I'll be careful with it," Russell promised. He looked at Fargo, who had explained the plan, and went on. "You'll need to find Caleb and tell him what's going on. He'll have to have at least two firemen for the boilers. More would be better."

"You know where I can find him?" Fargo asked.

Russell grinned. "Try the Snapping Turtle. It's a tavern down by the wharves."

Fargo nodded. He remembered seeing the place when the *Bayou Princess* docked a couple of days earlier.

"The timber and cotton I'm supposed to haul down to Shreveport was loaded today," Russell went on, "so we don't have to worry about that. We can leave first thing in the morning, as soon as it's light. I know that bayou about as well as anybody in these parts, but not even I would try to navigate it in the dark. The sandbars don't shift around much, like they do over in the Mississippi, but you never know when there might be a new snag that wasn't there before."

Fargo nodded. "First thing in the morning it is, then. I'll go find Thorn, and we'll start rounding up a crew. Probably be wise not to say anything about this to anyone, Captain. Maybe we can slip past McShane before he gets wind of it."

"Maybe," Russell said, but he didn't sound convinced. "That son of a buck's probably got spies here in Jefferson, though. Soon as we swing around in the Turning Basin in the morning, somebody will be on his way to McShane's camp."

"We'll deal with that when the time comes," Fargo said. In a way, he almost hoped that McShane *would* try to stop them. Like Cap'n Andy, he wouldn't mind another shot at the river pirates himself.

The Snapping Turtle was a squat building constructed of heavy timbers, located only a few yards from the edge of the bayou. Even though the hour was getting late, the tavern was still full of rivermen, drinking and playing cards and flirting with the serving girls in their long skirts and low-cut blouses. When Fargo came into the place, he looked around for Caleb Thorn, and true to Captain Russell's prediction, the one-legged old-timer was at a table in the corner, sitting by himself and nursing a drink.

Thorn looked up as Fargo approached, and a grin broke out on his weathered old face. "Good evenin' to you," he said as he gestured toward the empty chair on the other side of the table. "Sit down and have a drink with me, Fargo."

"I've got something more important to talk about than whiskey," Fargo said as he lowered himself onto the chair.

Thorn looked doubtful. "More important than whiskey? I ain't sure such a thing's been invented yet."

"How about making a run back down the bayou to Shreveport in the morning?"

Thorn's bushy white eyebrows rose in surprise. "I thought the cap'n was still laid up at the doctor's house."

"He's still recuperating," Fargo admitted, "but he wants to make the trip anyway. He'll navigate, and I'll handle the wheel. But we need you to tend to the boilers and the engines, and a couple of firemen, more if we can get them."

Thorn shook his head and said, "Everybody's scared o' Red Mike and his bunch. Traffic on the bayou ain't but about half o' what it used to be."

And that half was made up of boats whose captains

had contracts with Jonas Baxter, Fargo thought. Because they knew they were safe from the river pirates, even if they didn't know for certain about the link between Baxter and McShane.

"What about the men who were working on the *Bayou Princess* on the way up here?" Fargo asked.

Thorn shook his head again. "Both of 'em quit once we got to Jefferson. Said they didn't hanker to get shot at again anytime soon. You can't blame 'em for feelin' that way, neither."

"No," Fargo said. "I don't suppose you can. What about some of the other men?" He waved a hand at the crowd in the tavern. "Surely some of these hombres would like to have the work and aren't scared of McShane."

"Well, I guess I could ask around. . . ."

Fargo realized he had neglected an important point. "What about you, Caleb? Are *you* willing to make the trip?"

Thorn glared across the table at him. "I been with Cap'n Andy for about as many years as you been alive, mister. Ain't no bunch o' damned river rats gonna scare *me* off."

Fargo nodded. "I'm glad to hear it. Listen carefully, though. We need to keep it as quiet as possible about the boat leaving in the morning. So think hard before you ask anybody to sign on as part of the crew."

"You don't want word gettin' to McShane," Thorn guessed.

"That's right. We're hoping to slip past him before he knows we're on the bayou."

"I understand. I know a few ol' boys I'd trust to keep their mouths shut, even if they don't want the job. I'll find them and sound 'em out about it."

"That's exactly what we need you to do," Fargo said. "Thanks, Caleb."

"Save your thanks until we see whether or not I

can find anybody willin' to go along and likely get shot at."

Fargo stood up, clapped a hand on Thorn's bony old shoulder, then left the Snapping Turtle. He had put the plan in motion, but now there was something else he had to do.

He walked back over to Austin Street, to the Excelsior House. He didn't know if Isabel would still be awake, but she was not only awake; she must have been waiting for the sound of his footsteps, too, because she opened the door of her room as Fargo approached it, before he could knock.

"What happened, Skye?" she asked. "Those men Mr. Kiley was talking about . . . ?"

"Dead, all right," Fargo said. "And they were the ones who were bushwhacked by Dirkson this afternoon, too. So now there's nothing tying Dirkson and Baxter to the attack except me, and Sheriff Higgins says my word isn't good enough."

"He's as crooked as any of the rest of them," Isabel said.

Fargo nodded. "It's sure starting to look like it. That's why Kiley and I decided that I have to go to Shreveport and bring a U.S. marshal back here."

Her eyes widened in surprise. "You're leaving?"

"First thing in the morning on the *Bayou Princess*. We're going to make the run down there and back as fast as we can."

"But Cap'n Andy's in no shape to do something like that!"

"As long as he's got somebody else to handle the wheel, he ought to be all right," Fargo explained. "Even the doctor agreed with that, even though he wasn't too happy about it. So I'll be the helmsman, and Captain Russell won't have to do anything except navigate."

"If Red Mike finds out about this, he'll try to stop you."

"More than likely," Fargo agreed. "But we'll deal with that when the time comes. McShane won't take us by surprise, that's for sure."

Isabel drew in a deep, troubled breath. "I don't want to be selfish, Skye . . . but what about me? If Gideon knows that I'm here, I'll be in danger."

"Not if you stay here in the hotel until I get back. Don't let yourself get caught without plenty of people around. Unless Cutler's completely out of his mind, he won't try anything if he knows there'll be a lot of witnesses."

"Well, maybe." Isabel didn't sound convinced of that, however.

"With any luck I'll only be gone a couple of days, three at the most," Fargo said. He put his hands on her shoulders. "And as soon as there's some real law here in Jefferson, we'll deal with Cutler so that he'll never bother you again."

"I'm afraid Gideon may never give up, as long as he's alive." She moved against Fargo, molding her body to his. "But like you said about McShane, we'll deal with that when the time comes. Right now, since you'll be leaving in the morning, I want to make the best use of the time we still have together."

Fargo smiled. "I like the sound of that."

Isabel returned the smile, although the expression was a little strained with worry, as she said, "Then you'll like the sound of this, too." She came up on her toes, put her lips next to his ear, and whispered what she wanted to do the rest of the night.

Fargo's smile widened into a grin. Isabel was right. He *did* like the sound of that.

He got a little sleep that night. Not much, but enough, especially when he was fortified with a pre-dawn breakfast washed down with several cups of strong black coffee. He had left Isabel sleeping soundly, her head snuggled down into one of the pillows and her blond hair spread out around it, and he carried that image with him in his mind as he left the hotel and walked toward the waterfront, carrying his Henry rifle.

He wasn't *too* distracted by sweet memories, however. He knew he was still a threat to Baxter and Dirkson and was well aware they might try to eliminate him, so he kept his eyes open for any sort of ambush.

No one bothered him as he came up to the *Bayou Princess*. Lamps were burning on the riverboat, lighting it up in the early-morning gloom. A couple of men were stoking the firebox with pieces of cordwood from the big pile heaped on the deck just in front of the boilers. Fargo didn't recognize either of them, but he was prepared to put his trust in Caleb Thorn's judgment and accept them as part of the crew. He couldn't do much of anything else, under the circumstances.

Fargo crossed the broad gangplank to the deck and lifted a hand in greeting to Thorn, who came up the deck from the engines located in the stern, next to the big paddle wheel. The old-timer gestured toward the two firemen and said, "This here's Rollie Burnley and Jasper Milton. They're a mite long in the tooth, but they're hard workers."

"We ain't as old and decrepit as you, Caleb," one of the men said with a grin.

Fargo shook hands with the men and said, "You know you may be letting yourself in for some trouble?"

Tall, gangling Jasper Milton spat over the side into the bayou. "Let those blasted river pirates do their worst," he said. "Me an' Rollie ain't a-scared of 'em, are we, Rollie?"

"That's right," the shorter, stockier Burnley agreed. "We're anxious to show that we ain't ready to be put out to pasture just yet."

Fargo nodded, but he drew Thorn aside and said in a low voice to the engineer, "Let me guess. . . . None of the other riverboat captains will hire those two anymore—is that right?"

Thorn shrugged. "Stokin' a firebox is normally a job for younger fellas, but I've worked with Rollie and Jasper before. They won't let us down."

Fargo hoped Thorn was right. At this point, they didn't have any choice. They had to do the best they could with the help that was available.

"Nobody else wanted the job?"

Thorn shook his head. "Not with Red Mike and his bunch on the rampage."

"All right. Is Captain Russell already on board?"

"Up in the wheelhouse," Thorn replied, jerking a thumb in that direction.

Fargo climbed to the upper deck of the riverboat and entered the wheelhouse. Andy Russell, his wounded arm still in its sling, sat on a stool at the table, studying the charts spread out in front of him. He wore a blue jacket draped over the sling and a black river-man's cap on his head. He greeted Fargo with a curt nod and said, "We'll have steam up in about fifteen minutes. By then it'll be light enough to see what we're doing."

Fargo propped the Henry against the wall where it would be within easy reach as he stood at the wheel.

"You reckon you're gonna need that rifle?" Russell asked.

"I hope not," Fargo replied, "but I'd rather have it and not need it than need it and not have it."

Russell chuckled. "Those are words to live by, all right."

Fargo took the wheel, wrapping his fingers around the handles at the end of a couple of the spokes and getting used to the feel of it. Handling the big stern-wheeler was quite a responsibility, and he would be handling it by himself, without anyone to relieve him, since the *Bayou Princess* was operating with a skeleton crew. They might be able to pick up some more men in Shreveport, though, for the return trip.

Fargo looked through one of the wheelhouse windows toward the stable where he had left the Ovaro. He had gone by there on the way to the waterfront, and the Mexican liveryman had promised to take good care of the big stallion while Fargo was gone. Fargo and the Ovaro had been trail partners for a long time and had pulled each other through many a dangerous scrape. He would miss the big fella while he was gone on this trip down the bayou.

A few minutes later, Thorn reported through the speaking tube that the boilers had been heated up enough. They had steam up. Russell stood up and called back through the tube, giving the order to engage the engines. With the bayou widening out into the Turning Basin next to Jefferson's waterfront, there was no need to reverse the engines. The *Bayou Princess* simply pulled away from the timbered wharf, curving into the basin as the paddle wheel revolved faster and faster. In the wheelhouse, Russell told him how much to turn the big wheel, and the Trailsman followed the orders.

It took several minutes for the riverboat to turn around so that it was headed back down the bayou, and by that time people were gathering on the shore to watch it depart. Normally, the captain of a riverboat would let off a couple of blasts on the steam whistle to signal his intention of pulling out, but Russell hadn't done that. Still, despite the early hour, enough people were out and about so that the *Bayou Princess* had been unable to slip away unnoticed.

As Fargo glanced at the small crowd, he couldn't help but wonder if any of them were spies for Baxter and McShane. Even if none of them were, the word would spread quickly. A man on horseback could probably reach the river pirates' camp on Alligator

Slough before the stern-wheeler could steam past it. The likelihood was that trouble would be waiting for them somewhere along the way.

But at least the journey had gotten off to a good start. The air, while still humid, was cooler early in the morning, and the sky was a beautiful shade of pale blue, tinged with rose in the east where the sun was coming up. The steady chugging of the engines had a music of its own.

"Well, we're on our way," Captain Russell said.

Fargo nodded. "Yes. We're on our way."

And only time would tell what the voyage had in store for them.

11

The first couple of miles went past without any trouble. It didn't take long for Fargo to get a feel for the way the helm responded. Captain Russell moved his stool up next to the wheel so he could sit there and watch the bayou as it twisted and turned in front of them. His intimate knowledge of the stream made it possible for him to tell Fargo how to turn the wheel well in advance of the sandbars and other obstacles they wanted to avoid. Both men kept a close eye on the surface, watching for any snags. The sluggish current in the bayou meant that a jagged log could be lurking just under the water without causing a telltale ripple to warn the men on the riverboat.

While Fargo would never want to give up the mountains and the plains for an existence like this, he could understand how a life on the river could get into a man's blood. Even when you were traveling the same route, each bend of the river held the potential for something new. It was the same in a way with him, always wanting to see what was on the other side of every hill he came to. That restless nature was what had led him to the frontier.

"You think they'll be waiting for us at Alligator Slough?" he asked Russell.

The captain thought about it and said, "More than likely, they'll let us get past, then try the same sort of ambush they did before, with riflemen on the banks to slow us down and pirates in canoes coming up behind us. If they can get eight or ten men on board, that's enough to take over the boat."

"They won't be trying to loot the cargo," Fargo said. "This time their goal will be to wipe us out."

Russell nodded. "I know it." He pulled back the blue jacket he wore and revealed the butt of a revolver that was stuck through his belt. "There's nothing wrong with my right arm. I can still shoot a gun. Caleb and the other fellas are armed, too. We'll put up a fight—that's for damned sure."

Fargo knew that, but just putting up a fight wouldn't be enough. They had to win and reach Shreveport and the U.S. marshal, or Baxter would continue to get away with his campaign of murder and terror aimed at Lawrence Kiley.

By the time they neared Alligator Slough, Fargo had begun to recognize a few landmarks that warned him they were closing in on the likely spot of an ambush. Things looked a little different from the bayou than they did ashore, but Fargo's keen eyes took that into account. When he said something about that to Russell, the captain nodded.

"Yeah, the mouth of the slough's not more than half a mile ahead of us. If you need to use that rifle, Fargo, you go right ahead. I'll take the wheel one-handed if I have to."

"No, you won't," a voice said from behind them, in the open door of the wheelhouse.

Fargo had already heard a soft step on the stairs and started to turn. His face hardened into a grim mask as he saw Isabel Sterling standing there in the doorway. She wore man's trousers and a white shirt, and her hair was pulled back into a ponytail behind her head.

"Isabel!" Russell exclaimed. "What in blue blazes are you doing here?"

Fargo could have asked the same thing, but he

thought he already knew the answer. He said, "You stowed away, didn't you?"

She smiled. "I came on board while you were eating breakfast, Skye. I'm sorry I had to pretend to be asleep when you left. But I didn't want you and Cap'n Andy to have to make this trip alone. I thought I could help." She took a step into the wheelhouse. "Besides, I didn't want to stay there in Jefferson by myself. Not when Gideon might show up at any time."

"You mean Cutler, that no-good husband of yours?" Russell asked. "Has that varmint raised his ugly head again?"

Isabel nodded, her smile tinged with sadness and a little fear now. "Yes, I'm afraid so. I think he sent someone to track me down, and he knows where I am now."

"We can't be sure of that," Fargo pointed out.

"I wanted to be here with the two of you," Isabel said. "I'm sure of *that*."

"We ought to turn this boat around and head right back to Jefferson," Russell said.

"Don't you *dare*! I came to help, too, not just to run away from Gideon . . . again. If there's trouble, Skye can take care of it while you navigate, Cap'n Andy, and I'll take the wheel. That way you won't have to risk reinjuring your arm."

"Be a lot more to worry about than this ol' arm of mine if those river pirates take us over," Russell grumbled.

Isabel rested a hand on Fargo's shoulder. "That's not going to happen," she declared. "We won't let it. If it comes down to it, I can fight, too, as long as you've got an extra gun for me."

"Spare pistols and ammunition in the map cabinet." Russell shook his head gloomily. "Let's hope it don't come down to that."

That was Fargo's hope, all right. While they were talking to Isabel, the stern-wheeler had continued to steam on down the bayou. They had to be getting close to Alligator Slough by now, but so far there had been no sign of Red Mike McShane and his gang.

It was more likely, though, as Captain Russell had said, that the pirates wouldn't strike until after the *Bayou Princess* had gone past the slough. A few minutes later, the mouth of the smaller stream came in sight on the left. That was called port, Fargo reminded himself, since he was on a boat. The moss-draped trees sort of screened the entrance to the slough. Fargo watched it closely as the stern-wheeler paddled its way past. No canoes loaded with river pirates lurked in the shadowy tunnel formed by overhanging tree branches.

It was possible they had gotten there before the news of their departure from Jefferson reached McShane. Unlikely, but possible. Or maybe the pirates knew about it but hadn't had time to set up an ambush. Fargo didn't know. Either way, all he and his companions could do was press on.

Alligator Slough fell behind. Russell and Isabel heaved sighs of relief, but Fargo was still tense with worry as he stood at the wheel, his hands clasping it loosely at the moment. His eyes were always moving, scanning the banks along both sides of the bayou, searching for any signs of an ambush. The trees and brush were so thick that a small army could be hidden in them, and the people in the riverboat might not know about it until the bushwhackers opened fire.

Even though they had passed Alligator Slough, Fargo spotted several of the big reptiles sunning themselves on the banks up ahead. The gators could be found all up and down this bayou, as well as in Caddo Lake up ahead, not just in the slough that had been named for them.

"Take a couple of turns to starboard," Captain Russell said. "There's an old snag up here a couple of hundred yards."

Fargo turned the wheel, shifting his hands from grip

110

to grip as it revolved. The *Bayou Princess* began a ponderous swing to the right.

As it did, Fargo saw the alligators on the near bank suddenly lunge into the water with a swish of their muscular tails. The gators could have spotted a big fish or some other prey in the bayou they were going after. . . .

Or they could have been spooked into moving by the presence of some other predator in the brush near them.

And the most dangerous predator of all was man.

Fargo let go of the wheel and reached for his Henry rifle. "Take the wheel," he snapped at Isabel, grateful now that she was here. "And keep your head down!"

"Skye, what is it?" she asked, but even as she was speaking, she grabbed hold of the wheel as Fargo had told her.

"I'm not sure—" Fargo began as he lifted the rifle. Then a volley of shots roared out from the near bank. As Fargo crouched, he heard several of the bullets thud into the wall of the wheelhouse. Another slug passed directly through the open windows, coming in from the right and going out to the left without hitting anything. Fargo sensed as much as heard the low-pitched hum as the bullet passed close by his head.

Puffs of smoke from the brush marked the location of the bushwhackers. Fargo opened fire, cranking off four rounds as fast as he could work the Henry's loading lever. The growth was so thick that he couldn't tell if he hit anything, but he would have been willing to bet that he made at least one of the hidden riflemen duck for cover.

That didn't stop the shooting, though. Rifles started barking from the other bank, too. Fargo swiveled in that direction and loosed another three shots. He heard the crackle of pistols from down below and knew that Caleb Thorn, Rollie Burnley, and Jasper Milton were joining in on the fight.

111

Captain Russell, who was kneeling next to the chart table, turned his head to look out the rear window of the wheelhouse. "No canoes coming up behind us!" he reported, and that was one bit of good news, anyway, Fargo thought.

But they still had to run the gauntlet between the bushwhackers hidden in the forest bordering the bayou. Fargo swung around and threw some more lead to starboard.

"Trouble up ahead!" Isabel called out.

Biting back a curse, Fargo turned to look and saw a couple of canoes slicing toward the center of the stream, one from each bank, about fifty yards ahead. He frowned as he realized that they were empty. The pirates must have shoved the canoes out into the bayou, hoping to block the riverboat with them. But the *Bayou Princess* would just push the canoes aside without any trouble.

Then Fargo's blood turned to ice in his veins as he realized that the canoes weren't empty at all. True, no one was in them paddling.

But each canoe was occupied by two kegs of blasting powder.

Fargo grabbed the speaking tube and shouted, "Reverse! Reverse! Give it everything you've got!"

A mighty shudder ran through the riverboat as Caleb Thorn threw the engines out of gear and then into reverse. The big paddle wheel attached to the stern jerked and jolted to a stop. The action was so violent it felt as if the whole vessel was going to shake itself to pieces. But then the paddle wheel began to turn in the opposite direction.

That was the only chance of slowing down the boat enough for it to avoid the floating bombs up ahead. The *Bayou Princess* still had enough momentum, though, that it kept going forward even as the paddles churned the water and tried to hold it back. Fargo saw sparks flying in the air as fuses attached to the kegs burned closer and closer to the blasting powder.

He knew their time was up. He dropped the rifle, grabbed Isabel, and pulled her to the floor of the wheelhouse. At the same time he shouted to Russell, "Get down!"

The curved bow of the riverboat had just nudged between the booby-trapped canoes when the kegs of blasting powder exploded. The four blasts weren't simultaneous, but they were so close together they sounded almost like one.

The floor of the wheelhouse tilted for a second under Fargo and Isabel as the force of the explosion lifted the riverboat's bow out of the water and tore huge chunks from its hull. Fargo slid across the wheelhouse and crashed into the wall. Then the boat crashed back down into the water, throwing up a massive splash. The shattered bow plowed into the bottom of the shallow stream. The engines screamed, running away wildly as the angle of the vessel lifted the paddle wheel completely out of the bayou for a moment.

Fargo was stunned by the banging around he had received. He pushed himself up onto hands and knees and saw Isabel sprawled nearby. Russell was sitting up, propped against the map cabinet. His face was gray with pain, but Fargo didn't see any blood on the bandages around the captain's wounded arm, so that was good.

But that was about the only bit of good news, Fargo realized. He didn't know the extent of the damage the riverboat had suffered, but it wasn't moving anymore, and it might never move again.

He grabbed the Henry and surged to his feet. As he did so, a bullet buzzed past his ear. The men on the bank had emerged from cover and were raking the boat with rifle fire again. Fargo brought the Henry to his shoulder and snapped off a shot, sending one man plunging backward as Fargo's bullet smashed into his chest.

Pistol shots still sounded on the lower decks, proving that somebody was still alive down there and putting up a fight. But the defenders of the *Bayou Princess* were heavily outnumbered, and the boat itself was a sitting duck in the water. More canoes, these filled with river pirates, put out into the bayou, and the men on the banks laid down volley after volley of covering fire. Fargo was forced to dive to the floor as slugs began to punch their way through the bullet-riddled, weakened walls of the wheelhouse.

"Stay down!" he told Isabel and Russell.

A moment later, the guns fell silent. Fargo heard the heavy sound of boots on the deck, followed by a flurry of gunshots, then more silence. He knew the pirates had boarded the boat.

"Stay here," he grated as he came up in a crouch. He kicked the wheelhouse door open and saw a couple of roughly dressed men starting up the stairs. He recognized one of them as Linus McShane, Red Mike's brother. Fargo fired the Henry, hitting the other man, who was slightly in front of Linus. The river pirate howled in pain and fell back, the arm that Fargo had just drilled flopping uselessly as blood welled from it.

Linus emptied the pistol he held in Fargo's direction, forcing the Trailsman to duck back to avoid the hail of bullets. A second later, a voice that he recognized as belonging to Red Mike shouted, "Hold your fire, Fargo! Hold your fire, damn it!"

Fargo stayed where he was, covering the part of the stairway he could see.

"You hear me, Fargo?" Red Mike called. "You better talk to me!"

"I hear you!" Fargo shouted back. "What do you want?"

"You and whoever's up there with you better throw

114

out your guns and surrender! You can't get off this boat!"

"Surrender and let ourselves be killed, you mean?"

"You won't be hurt!" McShane insisted. "You got my word on that."

"Yeah, your word means a whole lot after you've tried to blow us up and shot at us a couple of hundred times!"

Fargo heard McShane chuckle, of all things. "Yeah, that trick with the blasting powder in the canoes was a pretty good'un, wasn't it? If you hadn't been able to slow that boat down a little, it would've been blowed to pieces, and maybe you along with it. So you're right—I wanted you dead. But now that I think about it, I've changed my mind."

That puzzled Fargo, and he didn't know whether to believe Red Mike or not. And there was also the question of whether or not he and his companions would be any better off as prisoners of the river pirates.

But even as he asked himself that, he knew the answer. They were outnumbered and couldn't escape, which meant that if they continued to fight, sooner or later the pirates would storm the wheelhouse and kill him and Captain Russell. They might just take Isabel captive if they could, but she would eventually die, too, when they got tired of abusing her.

But as long as he still lived, there was hope. He had won out against seemingly overwhelming odds in the past.

Even though Fargo was already leaning in the direction of surrendering—for the moment—McShane tipped the scales by adding, "Throw out your guns, or these three old fools will die, Fargo. You got my word on *that*, too."

Fargo risked a look and saw Caleb Thorn, Rollie Burnley, and Jasper Milton down on the hurricane deck, surrounded by McShane's men. All of them had blood on their clothes, but they were standing straight and didn't seem to be hurt too badly. All McShane had to do was give the order, though, and his men would riddle them.

Fargo glanced at Isabel and Russell. "What do you think?" he asked them in a quiet voice.

"The *Princess* is hard aground," Russell said. "I could tell that by the way it felt when she came to a stop. She won't be going anywhere soon, and maybe never again if those explosions did enough damage. Seems to me that we don't have much choice." If he hadn't looked pained already, that admission probably would have caused the grimace that came over his strained features. "Besides, I don't want anything else happening to my crew."

Isabel swallowed hard. "I agree, Skye. Red Mike will murder us all if he's forced into it. Maybe if we pretend to cooperate, we'll have a chance later to escape."

Fargo's mouth was a grim line. Giving up stuck in his craw. Always had and always would . . . but maybe not for much longer, depending on how things worked out here.

He might not live long enough to worry about it.

"All right," he called to Red Mike. "You win, McShane! We're coming out!"

"Throw all your guns out first!" McShane ordered.

Fargo laid the Henry on the floor and gave it a push, sliding it out the door. He heard the clatter as the rifle fell down the steep stairway. He followed it with his Colt and the pistol Russell had, then tossed out his Arkansas toothpick last.

"Is that it?" McShane asked.

"That's all," Fargo replied. There were guns in the map cabinet, the captain had said, but none of those weapons had been broken out during the fight.

"Then come ahead!"

Fargo got to his feet and helped Russell up. "How's the arm?" he asked.

"It just hurts from being banged around. I don't think it started bleeding again."

Fargo nodded. He held on to Russell's good arm to steady the captain as they emerged from the wheel-house and started down the stairs. Isabel followed close behind them.

At least a dozen guns were pointed at them as they reached the hurricane deck at the bottom of the stair-way. McShane grinned and said, "You should've known better, Fargo. This bayou belongs to me. No-body travels up or down it without my say-so."

"Things may not always be that way," Fargo snapped.

"I wouldn't count on it." McShane turned to his men. "Put them in the canoes and take them ashore. Keep a close eye on them, especially Fargo here. I got a feelin' that he's a tricky one." The boss of the river pirates chuckled again. "If he tries anything, throw one of those old-timers in the bayou. I'll bet the gators are hungry. They always are."

12

Once the prisoners had been taken ashore, they were marched through the woods at gunpoint, surrounded by the river pirates. Fargo was able to talk to Caleb Thorn, Rollie Burnley, and Jasper Milton and found that while all three members of the crew had been nicked by flying lead, none of them had serious injuries. Captain Russell was still gray-faced from the pain of his wounded arm, but it wasn't bleeding and he seemed fairly strong.

Isabel trudged along beside Fargo. She asked in a half whisper, "Why didn't they kill us?"

"I don't know," Fargo replied with a shake of his head. "They were certainly trying hard enough to there for a while."

That same question nagged at him. When Baxter found out that Fargo had left Jefferson, he must have figured Fargo was on his way to Shreveport to fetch the U.S. marshal. His orders to McShane would have been to stop the *Bayou Princess* and kill Fargo. Considering that trick with the kegs of blasting powder in the canoes, that had been McShane's intent.

But when that failed, at least where killing Fargo was concerned, and the river pirates had had to fight their way onto the boat, McShane had changed his mind for some reason. Fargo pondered on what that reason might be, but he couldn't come up with an answer.

The pirates knew these woods well enough to cut across country and get back to their camp on Alligator Slough. When they arrived and the prisoners were marched in, a couple of older men who had been left behind and several women, including the slatternly-looking blonde with the scar on her face, looked on with interest.

"Lock 'em in the smokehouse, Linus," McShane ordered his brother.

Linus nodded and gave Fargo a hard shove that almost made the Trailsman stumble. "Get goin', you," Linus said. "I ain't forgot that you nearly shot me, so don't give me no trouble or you'll be sorry."

"Take it easy, Linus," McShane said. "I don't want any of them hurt . . . yet."

Linus grumbled at that reprimand, but he herded Fargo and the others into a small, sturdy log building. All the chinks between the logs had been filled with mud that was allowed to dry in place, so not much air could get in or out. Inside, a fire pit had been dug in the ground. The smoke from mostly smothered flames was used to cure meat that was hung up inside the shack. While the heavy door was open and some light penetrated the single room, Fargo saw several carcasses hanging inside. They had been feral hogs before they were slaughtered.

He felt a little like he and his companions were being led to the slaughter, too.

But McShane had reiterated that he wanted the prisoners kept alive for now. At this point, all Fargo could do was be patient and bide his time. Answers— and an opportunity to escape—might come later.

Once the door had slammed shut and was barred from outside, the prisoners had nothing to do except sit down inside the gloomy structure and try to conserve their strength. Fargo sat with his back propped against the wall, Isabel on one side of him and Russell on the other. Nobody talked much. Fargo sensed that an air of despondency gripped the others, especially Isabel. She had tried to escape the danger posed by her husband, only to fall into even greater peril.

Fargo wasn't going to despair, though. He might be a captive now, but he never gave up hope, not as long as he was still drawing breath.

Time dragged by. Despite the chinking between the logs, a few tiny gaps remained here and there, and enough light filtered in to prove it was still daylight outside. Fargo studied the inside of the smokehouse. There was no ceiling, only the bare beams and rafters that held up the roof.

After what seemed like an eternity, the faint glow began to dim even more, and Fargo knew that twilight was settling down over the forest. His empty stomach confirmed that. He hadn't eaten since breakfast in the Excelsior House dining room early that morning, and that had been a long time ago. Rollie Burnley had mentioned something about tearing a hunk off one of the hog carcasses with his bare hands, but Fargo had advised against it. The meat hadn't been smoked yet and would probably make them deathly ill if they ate any of it.

Eventually it was completely dark inside the smokehouse, but then a short time later, a reddish glow appeared in the gaps between the logs. Fargo sat up straighter as he heard the bar being lifted from the door. It swung open, and the glare from a couple of torches spilled into the building.

After hours of being locked up in there, the prisoners squinted against the torchlight. As Fargo's eyes began to adjust, he made out the figures of several pirates standing outside the door, including Linus McShane. A couple of the men held torches while the others pointed rifles and pistols at the captives.

The scarred blonde was with the pirates. She held a burlap sack in her hands. As she stepped just inside the door, she tossed it on the ground and said, "Here. Red Mike don't want you starvin' to death."

Burnley and Milton grabbed the bag. Burnley opened it, and Milton took hard biscuits from it and started passing them around to the others.

Fargo expected the woman to step out and shut the door again, but she lingered for a few seconds, until Linus snapped, "Come on, Tillie. You done what Mike said to do. Let's go."

The blonde nodded. She backed out of the smoke-house and swung the door shut.

Even as it closed, though, Fargo still felt Tillie's gaze on him.

Around the hunk of biscuit Isabel had gnawed off, she said, "That bitch was certainly giving you the eye, Skye."

"Really?" Fargo murmured. "I didn't notice."

He began eating one of the biscuits and thought about what had just happened. Despite what he'd said to Isabel, he had been well aware of how the blonde was studying him. He didn't know if that was because she found him attractive—or if she was thinking about the best way to kill him.

There were enough biscuits in the sack to satisfy the hunger of the prisoners, or at least blunt it. More time passed, and Fargo heard snores coming from some of the others. Exhaustion had claimed them.

Then the reddish glare of the torches returned and the door was opened again. Fargo didn't see any sign of Tillie this time, but Linus had returned, along with several other men. They covered the prisoners with rifles as Linus said, "All right, Fargo, come out of there."

His tone made it clear that he hoped Fargo would argue, so he would have an excuse to use force. Instead, Fargo pushed himself to his feet, ignoring the protests of muscles that were stiff from sitting for so long.

Isabel caught hold of his hand. "Skye . . . ?"

He smiled down at her. "Don't worry," he said. "If they wanted to hurt us, they would've done it before now. I'll see what Red Mike wants."

Linus sneered and asked, "How do you know I ain't the one who wants to talk to you?"

Fargo regarded him coolly and said, "Because I know your brother is the one who gives the orders around here."

Linus's face flushed with anger and resentment, just as Fargo had intended. It never hurt to try to drive a wedge, even a small one, between one's enemies.

He walked out of the smokehouse. With the river pirates all around him and the barrel of Linus's rifle prodding him in the back, he walked over to one of the cabins. When he went in, he saw Red Mike McShane sitting at a rough-hewn table with a bottle of whiskey in front of him. Tillie stood on the other side of the room. She acted like she wasn't paying any attention to what was going on, but Fargo saw her shoot a glance in his direction.

McShane pointed to an empty chair on the other side of the table and said, "Sit down, Fargo. Want a drink?"

"I wouldn't mind," Fargo said as he sat. McShane pushed the bottle across the table. Fargo picked it up and took a healthy slug of the fiery liquor. It was raw stuff, but it sent a bracing heat through his veins.

"You've been a damn problem ever since you showed up in these parts," McShane went on. "I should've just gone ahead and killed you the way the boss wanted, I reckon. But it occurred to me it might come in handy to keep you alive for a while."

"Not that I don't appreciate that sentiment," Fargo said, "but I'm curious why you feel that way."

McShane grinned and leaned forward to snag the bottle. He took a drink, too, and said, "Leverage."

Understanding dawned on Fargo. "You want a bigger piece of the pie," he said. "As long as I'm alive, you can hold the threat of me testifying against him over Baxter's head. And you can threaten the other prisoners to get me to do what you want."

"Yeah." McShane laughed. "You got some of that right, anyway."

Fargo wasn't sure what he meant by that. The confusion didn't last long, though, because he heard the sound of hooves outside, and a moment later one of the pirates stuck his head in the door and announced, "She's here, Mike, like you wanted."

McShane nodded and stood up. "Good."

The man at the door stepped aside, and a woman walked into the cabin. She was dressed in a dark green riding skirt and jacket. She stopped short just inside the door and stared at Fargo in surprise and anger. A stylish flat-crowned hat with a strap that tied under her chin was perched on her auburn curls.

"My God," Francine Baxter said. "What's he doing here?"

Fargo looked from Francine to Red Mike and back again, and now he knew why Francine had looked familiar to him when he first saw her the night before. He had noticed the family resemblance between her and the McShane brothers. There was no doubt in his mind now that Francine was their sister.

"I'm tired of doin' your lover's dirty work for nothing but what we can steal off those riverboats," Red Mike snapped. "You wouldn't be close to takin' over the timber business in these parts if it wasn't for the way me and Linus and the boys have made life hell for Kiley. I want a slice of those profits, too."

Fargo's brain worked swiftly, taking in what McShane had just said and figuring all the implications of it. Before Francine could respond to her brother's demand, Fargo made a guess and said, "Dirkson won't like that. I'm betting he won't go along with it, either."

Francine stared at him again. "How did you—" She stopped, but her reaction had already confirmed Fargo's theory that she and Nick Dirkson were the masterminds behind the trouble, not her husband, Jonas Baxter. Fargo realized that he had misjudged the man. Baxter might be a ruthless, prickly son of a bitch, but from the looks of things, he wasn't in league with the river pirates after all. Red Mike had tipped Fargo off to that with his use of the term "your lover" instead of "your husband," as he would have said to Francine if he had meant Baxter.

"Look, there's no point in arguing," Red Mike said. "Fargo knows what's going on."

"He does *now*, you damned fool!" Francine burst out. "He thought Jonas was behind everything! We planned all along for any blame to fall on Jonas, and now you've ruined it!"

Red Mike frowned. He was probably realizing that in his avarice, he had misplayed the hand. But it was too late to back out of this power grab now, so he said, "None of that matters. Tell Dirkson he's gonna have to cut me in for a bigger share, or I'll turn Fargo loose to go to the law."

"You're wanted, too, you know," Francine said in an icy voice.

McShane shrugged. "We can be long gone from these parts before any posse could ever find us. There are plenty of other places where we can hide out and pull jobs. The pickin's might even be better someplace else. But you and Dirkson won't be sittin' so pretty anymore."

Francine stalked over to the table and snatched up the whiskey bottle. "Let me think about this," she snapped. She brought the bottle to her lips, tilted her head back, and took a long swallow.

Fargo wondered how Jonas Baxter had wound up married to a woman like her. More than likely, Baxter didn't know that his wife's brothers were river pirates. Francine must have escaped from a bad background by marrying a wealthy man like Baxter, and when she had grown tired of him and begun an affair with Nick Dirkson, it had occurred to her to call in her brothers to help the two of them take over Baxter's timber business. First, though, they wanted to eliminate the competition, in the form of Lawrence Kiley, and make Baxter's operation even more valuable.

Fargo didn't know if he was guessing correctly about every nuance of the scheme, but he was willing to bet things had followed those general lines. Probably only a few of Baxter's men were in on the plan, including the one who had provided the supplies to the river pirates.

"You're threatening to cut off your own nose to spite your face—you know that, don't you?" Francine said to Red Mike.

He just laughed. "I've told you the deal."

"All right," she said. "Nick won't like it, but I can get him to go along with it. You've got to do a couple of things for me, though."

"Like what?"

"I'm tired of waiting for Kiley to give up. I want you to hit his main camp tonight and wipe it out. Kill everybody there."

Francine gave the order for mass murder without even a tinge of emotion in her voice.

Red Mike thought about it for a second and then nodded. "I reckon we can do that. What else do you want?"

Francine turned her head to nod toward Fargo. "Kill him."

"Not just yet. That can wait until we're done with the other. Just to make sure you ain't tryin' to pull any tricks on us, little sis."

"Good Lord! Have I ever double-crossed you?"

"No . . . but I don't intend for there to be a first time, neither."

"All right," she snapped. "Hit Kiley's camp and then kill Fargo. But don't let me down, Mike."

"I won't. You can count on it."

Francine took another slug of the whiskey. She was a little more relaxed as she said, "When you sent for me tonight, I never dreamed things were going to start moving this fast."

"We've waited long enough to be rich," McShane said. "When we were all growin' up, back there in Tennessee, I told you we'd have money someday."

"Yeah, but you figured I'd earn it for you and Linus by whoring."

Red Mike chuckled. "Well, since you was so good at it, seemed like all that talent shouldn't go to waste."

She leaned closer to him, and even though she was smiling, Fargo saw that her eyes were like chips of green ice. "I should've cut your throat while you were sleeping, you and Linus's both. I was fourteen."

"Yeah, but you didn't, and look at you know. A rich lady, fixin' to get richer. Hell, it's only a matter of time until that husband of yours has himself a little accident, ain't it?"

"We'll see," Francine said. "We'll see."

Everything Fargo had seen and heard in this cabin tonight made him feel a little sick to his stomach, but he had kept his face expressionless, even when they were talking about killing him. Francine probably didn't know about the other prisoners, but that didn't matter. Her brothers would get rid of them, too, at the same time Fargo was killed.

That meant he had until the men got back from the raid on Kiley's camp to figure out a way to escape.

"I'm going back to town," Francine said. "You'll send word when everything's taken care of?"

"Sure. By tomorrow morning, some of your problems will be over and done with. Just make sure Dirkson doesn't kick up a fuss."

She gave a snort of disdain. "Nick will do whatever I want him to. He thinks he's running things, but we both know he's really not."

"Yeah, you always did like to be the boss."

Francine gave him another cold-eyed stare and then left, turning on her heel to walk out of the cabin. Linus came in after she was gone and asked his brother, "You and Frannie get everything worked out?"

"Yeah. Take Fargo back to the smokehouse and lock him up again, then get all the boys together. We're gonna hit Kiley's main camp tonight. Time for all them timber jacks to die. When we get back, we'll get rid of the prisoners."

Linus nodded, equally undisturbed by the idea of mass murder. He came over to the table, grabbed Fargo's arm, and jerked him roughly to his feet.

"Come on," Linus grated. "Better enjoy your last night, Fargo. Come mornin', you and the others'll be breakfast for some happy gators."

He gave Fargo a shove that propelled him through the door. Fargo stumbled a little but caught his balance. A glance told him that he was surrounded by rifle-toting river pirates, so there was no chance to make a break. They took him back to the smokehouse. He went inside and stood there listening to the sound of the bar being lowered into place.

"Skye, thank God you're back," Isabel said. "I didn't know if we would ever see you again."

"McShane didn't plan to kill me," Fargo told her. "Not yet, anyway. But later . . . that's another story."

"Better tell us, Fargo," Captain Russell said.

Fargo agreed. He spent several minutes explaining everything he had learned tonight. Isabel gasped in surprise when she heard that Francine Baxter was the sister of Red Mike and Linus McShane.

"I saw her in Jefferson several times," Isabel said. "She always seemed like such a lady."

"It was a good act, all right," Fargo agreed. "From the sound of it, though, she's the one who came up with all the plans, like trying to ruin Kiley's business by scaring off the riverboat captains with those attacks by her brothers."

Russell said, "There are probably guards out at Kiley's logging camp, but they won't be expecting an all-out raid like that. They'll be wiped out."

Fargo nodded. "Unless somebody manages to warn them."

"Like one of us?" Caleb Thorn said. "How in blazes can we do that when we're locked up tighter'n a drum in here?"

Fargo didn't answer. Instead he felt around in the darkness until he found the empty sack that the biscuits had been in. It was burlap, and fairly tough. But he was able to gnaw a place along the edge and start the fabric separating, and once he had done that he could rip the burlap into strips. He did so, then working in the dark by feel he knotted the strips together until he had a makeshift rope about a dozen feet long.

Fargo stood up. He held one end of the rope and flipped the other upward, toward the roof. He was casting blindly, and it took him several tries before the rope didn't fall back to his feet. He waved his other arm in front of him, found the dangling rope, and took hold of it so that he could tug hard on both ends.

The rope held. He had succeeded in tossing it over one of the beams. Now if it would just support his weight . . .

Fargo had seen earlier in the day that the beams were too high to reach, even with a couple of the other prisoners giving him a boost. He had noted as well that there were a few gaps between the boards on the roof.

Burnley and Milton were both wounded, but not

seriously, and they were younger than Caleb Thorn and Captain Russell. Fargo said, "Rollie, Jasper, come over here."

"What do you want, Fargo?" Burnley said.

"Cup your hands and give me a boost. I've got a rope looped over one of those beams, and with you two helping me, I think I can pull myself up into the rafters."

"What good's that gonna do?" Milton asked.

"The roof is made of planks, not logs," Fargo explained. "I think I can maybe work one or two of them loose."

"Sounds like it might work," Burnley admitted.

"Worth a try, anyway," Milton said.

"Skye, be careful," Isabel put in. "If any of those pirates figures out what you're doing, they're liable to come in here and hurt you."

"They're planning to kill us in the morning when they get back from that raid," Fargo pointed out. "I think a little risk tonight is worth it."

Again working by feel, Burnley and Milton joined their hands to form crude stirrups for Fargo's feet. He hung on to the burlap rope as they lifted him. Then he began pulling himself upward, hand over hand. The rough burlap burned his palms as his weight hit them, but he didn't lose his grip.

After a moment, when he reached up, his fingers brushed the rough wood of the beam. He clung to it, looped his other arm over it, pulled himself higher, and kicked a leg upward, flinging it over the beam as well. From there he was able to lift and roll himself on top of it.

Fargo got hold of a rafter and climbed higher. He rested both feet on the beam and balanced himself. The roof was low enough so that he had to crouch almost double, even at its highest point. He felt along the underside of the roof, searching for a gap between boards.

It took him several minutes to locate a crack wide enough for him to slip his fingers through it. When he did, though, he grasped the board and began to put pressure on it, working it back and forth. It had a little play. Not much, but enough to give him hope. The river pirates had thrown up the buildings in their camp hurriedly, and they hadn't done a very good job of it.

Fargo had to go slow. He didn't want the screech of nails being pulled free to alert the guards. But after a while his steady efforts began to pay off. The board loosened even more. Fargo kept working at it, encouraged by his progress but all too aware that time was passing. Most of the pirates had probably left the camp by now to attack the loggers who worked for Lawrence Kiley. The chances of being able to warn the men in time were dwindling.

The board came loose. Fargo angled it and brought it inside through the opening he had created. He lowered it to the men below, who felt around in the darkness until they got hold of it and took it from him. Now Fargo had enough space to get both hands on the next board and start to prize it up.

Again, the work was slow and tedious, but when the second board finally came free, Fargo was able to wedge himself through the opening he had made. He pulled himself up onto the roof and sprawled there for a moment, listening intently. He was on the back side of the roof. He crawled up to its peak and looked over. A fire still burned in the center of the pirates' camp, casting a flickering glow over the cabins. Fargo didn't see anyone moving around. That confirmed his theory that the gang had already left on the raid. He heard a cough at the front of the smokehouse and knew at least one guard had to be stationed there. Fargo began sliding forward toward the front edge of the roof.

When he was close enough to peer over the edge,

he saw a man sitting there on a tree stump. The man had a rifle across his knees and was trying to roll a quirly. Moving quietly, Fargo drew himself up in a crouch and then launched from the top of the smokehouse in a diving tackle.

The guard jerked his head up, but not in time to avoid Fargo's attack. They crashed together. The impact drove the guard backward off the stump. Fargo landed on top, clubbed his hands together, and smashed them down into the guard's face. The man went limp, knocked senseless by the powerful blow, maybe even dead.

Fargo was reaching for the rifle the guard had dropped when a woman's shrill voice said, "Hold it! One more move and I'll blow you to pieces, mister!"

Fargo looked up and saw Tillie, the scarred blonde, standing no more than ten feet away, a shotgun in her hands.

And she held the Greener like she knew how to use it.

13

At this range, if Tillie pulled the triggers of that double-barreled weapon, the twin charges of buckshot would turn Fargo into something that looked only vaguely human. He tried to keep the strain out of his voice as he said, "Take it easy, Tillie. I don't mean you any harm."

"How about Red Mike?" she demanded with a sneer. "You mean him any harm?"

Fargo's answer was honest. "I want to stop him from killing Kiley's men."

"That ain't good enough," Tillie said. Then she lowered the shotgun a little. "I want you to kill him."

The words took Fargo by surprise, but he remained calm as he said, "How about if I stand up and we talk about this?"

"All right. Just don't try any tricks. I don't know how you got out of that smokehouse, but the fact that you did tells me you're a dangerous man."

"Not to you," Fargo said as he pushed himself to his feet without picking up the rifle. "I don't have anything against you. My quarrel is with the McShane brothers."

"Fine. I ain't overfond of those bastards, neither." She let go of the shotgun with her left hand and raised it to her scarred cheek. "Red Mike gave me this, 'cause he told me to bed down with his brother and

I didn't want to. Linus sometimes likes to hurt the girls he's with. But then, I reckon Mike's the same way. Both of 'em are no better'n animals. And that sister o' theirs is the worst of all. Wouldn't think it to look at her, would you?"

Fargo shook his head. "You can't always judge a person by how they look. Hell, you usually can't judge them that way."

"Yeah. I was just on my way to let you folks out. Wouldn't have thought that, would you?"

"No," Fargo replied. "I didn't think you'd be brave enough to cross Red Mike that way. But I'm glad I was wrong about you."

Tillie snorted. "Don't get the idea I'm goin' soft. I just want Red Mike and Linus dead, that's all, and you look like the sort of gent who could get that done. Now *I'm* the one judgin' by appearances, I guess. Can you do it?"

"I don't often set out to kill someone, no matter what they've done," Fargo told her. "But if they put up a fight—and they will—I sure as blazes won't hold back."

Tillie nodded. "That's good enough for me. All your guns and that big knife o' yours are all in the cabin where you talked to Mike and his sister earlier. You can go get them whilst I let the others out."

"All right." Fargo paused before he went to retrieve the weapons, though. "How were you going to get past the guard?"

Tillie reached in her pocket and brought out a wicked-looking straight razor. "Ol' Lonnie there would've let me get behind him. He wouldn't have suspected a thing until it was too late and his throat was sliced open."

Fargo didn't doubt for a second that she would have done it, too. It was probably lucky for Lonnie, assuming he was still alive, that Fargo had jumped him first.

No one else seemed to be in the camp as Fargo

hurried over to Red Mike's cabin. It was possible that McShane had taken all the men except Lonnie with him to Kiley's logging camp. The handful of women besides Tillie had to still be around, but they were probably lying low in the other cabins. No one challenged Fargo as he retrieved the weapons, and that was the main thing.

Isabel, Captain Russell, and the other three men had emerged from the smokehouse by the time Fargo got back there. As Fargo handed out the guns, he said, "Tillie was going to let us go anyway. She's not really one of the gang."

Isabel sniffed. "You were about to rescue us, Skye. I don't see that we owe her anything."

"No?" Tillie said. "How about Fargo's life? I had the drop on him with a scattergun and could've blown him from hell to breakfast."

"That's true," Fargo said with a wry grin.

"Well," Isabel admitted, "I guess we should feel a *little* grateful."

Lonnie had regained consciousness, Fargo noted, so he wasn't dead after all. One of the others had tied his hands behind his back with his own belt. As he glared up at Fargo, he blustered, "Red Mike's gonna skin you alive, mister."

Fargo ignored the threat. He turned to Russell and asked, "Do you know how to get to Kiley's camp, Cap'n?"

"I think so," Russell said. "I was out there once. But I don't know these woods near as well as I know the bayou."

"Just get us close," Fargo said with a nod. "Then I reckon the sound of gunfire will lead us the rest of the way."

Moving through the forest at night wasn't easy, especially for people who didn't really know where they were going. They had to cut across country, which made things even more difficult. But there was no time to follow Alligator Slough to Big Cypress Bayou and then follow the bayou back to Jefferson. If they had tried to do that, Kiley's men would have been wiped out long before they could reach the logging camp.

So Fargo had to rely on instinct and occasional glimpses of the stars to guide them. Captain Russell had told him that Kiley's camp was northeast of the settlement, so Fargo steered them in that direction as best he could. He had found some hatchets in the pirates' camp, and the group used those to chop their way through the underbrush. When they came to a clearer stretch every now and then, they broke into a trot until the vegetation closed in around them again.

Also, before leaving the camp on Alligator Slough, Tillie had told Fargo that she wouldn't be there whenever anybody got back, whether it was Fargo who returned or Red Mike and the rest of the pirates.

"My time here is done," she said. "But I'm leavin' holdin' you to your word, Fargo. You got to kill Red Mike and Linus."

Fargo hadn't exactly promised her that he would kill the McShane brothers, but that was probably what a showdown would come to. The pirates weren't the sort of men to surrender and face justice in the courts. They would rather take their chances with hot lead.

Fargo didn't really want to take Isabel into battle with him, but neither did he think it would be a good idea to leave her behind at the pirates' camp. Besides, she never would have agreed to that. She was too much of a fighter for that.

"I wish I'd had it out with Gideon, instead of running away," she told Fargo as they made their way through the thickets with the others strung out behind them. "I guess I didn't know then how strong I really am."

"It takes a while to figure that out sometimes," Fargo agreed. "The important thing is that you know it now."

"That's right, and I'll never run from him again. I almost hope he *has* found me, because I don't want that hanging over my head anymore."

Fargo knew what she meant. In his experience, it was usually better to confront trouble head-on.

A short time later, he stopped as the distant crackle of gunfire came to his ears. "Listen," he said to the others.

"Sounds like a war," Russell said. "Too bad we didn't get there in time to warn those fellas."

"That just wasn't possible. But it sounds like they're putting up quite a fight. Maybe we can change the odds a little if we get there in time."

Fargo started moving again, stepping up the pace. A few minutes later he stumbled a little as he broke out of the brush into a broad, open space. It was another skid road, he realized, and it would lead them right to the logging camp. He turned toward the sound of shots and broke into a run. The others hurried after him.

He had his own Henry rifle in his hands and his Colt snugged in the holster on his hip. Having the weapons back made him feel more comfortable about going into battle. The fighting spirit that was always within him soared.

He began to see muzzle flashes up ahead. Charging right into the middle of a fight without knowing what was going on was a good way to get killed, so Fargo slowed his charge and motioned for the others to slow down as well. The six of them gathered in the darkness to study the situation.

The skid road led to a large clearing, in which a long, low building had been constructed from logs. That would be the logging crew's bunkhouse, Fargo knew. A few shacks were scattered around. One of them would be the cookshack; the others probably were used for storage of tools and supplies. Shots came from inside the bunkhouse as the loggers defended the place. More muzzle flashes from the surrounding woods gave away the positions of the attackers.

"Stay here," Fargo told his companions in a low voice. "I'm going to try to pick off some of those pirates before they know what's going on. The rest of you hit the others from behind when I give you the signal."

Isabel clutched at his arm and said again, "Be careful, Skye." This time she reinforced the warning by tugging him closer and giving him a hard kiss on the mouth.

Burnley chuckled. "If that don't give a fella a good reason to stay alive, I don't know what would."

Fargo knew exactly what he meant. He was looking forward to a time when all this trouble would be over, when he and Isabel could be alone together again.

But for now there was deadly business to take care of. He squeezed her shoulder and then moved off into the night, disappearing into the shadows of the trees at the edge of the skid road.

This wasn't the first time Fargo had engaged in such clandestine warfare. As silently and swiftly as an Indian, he slipped through the forest, letting the sounds of gunfire guide him. His eyes had adjusted to the darkness, and he was able to make out the shape of a man crouched behind a pine tree, firing at the bunkhouse. Fargo stepped up to him, lifted the Henry, and slammed the rifle butt into the back of his head with one smooth, powerful stroke.

The blow had enough force behind it to knock the man senseless but not enough to shatter his skull. Fargo didn't kill in cold blood unless he was absolutely forced to. The man went down without uttering a sound. Fargo knelt beside him, felt for a belt, but didn't find one. He used his Arkansas toothpick to cut strips from the man's shirt and used those to bind his hands and feet tightly enough so that he couldn't get loose. Then he crammed another piece of shirt in the man's mouth as a gag.

From there it was on to the next man. Fargo slipped up on him and knocked him out and tied him up the same way. He had just taken a third man out of the fight in the same manner when a sudden flare of light caught his attention. He twisted toward it and saw a torch spinning through the air toward the bunkhouse. It was a crude affair, just a broken branch with dried moss wrapped around one end, but the moss burned easily and the torch made an effective weapon. It landed on the bunkhouse roof and continued to blaze.

Several other torches joined it a moment later, then a half dozen more rained down out of the night and landed on the roof. The pirates were going to burn the loggers out, force them to flee from the burning building and shoot them down as they tried to escape from the flames.

Fargo couldn't do anything about the fire. It was too late for that. The only chance the defenders had was for Fargo and his companions to provide them with a distraction so they could get clear of the building.

"Now!" Fargo shouted toward the skid road where he had left the others. "Hit them now!"

Not too far off, a man yelled, "What the hell! Fargo!"

That sounded like one of the McShanes, Fargo thought. He pivoted in that direction, brought the Henry to his shoulder, and fired twice, aiming at the sound of the voice. An orange flower of muzzle flame bloomed in the darkness as whoever it was returned the fire. Fargo threw himself to one side and triggered the Henry again as bullets whipped past him.

He heard a strangled cry, and a second later, as he

surged to his feet again, Linus McShane stumbled into view. The roof of the bunkhouse was on fire now, and the glare from the fire reached into the trees, lighting them up like a nightmarish scene from some crazed artist's vision of a woodland hell. Linus pawed at his throat as blood spilled darkly from the wound that one of Fargo's bullets had torn there. Gargling and choking on his own blood, Linus pitched forward and shuddered his way into death as he lay on the ground.

Half of Tillie's goal had been accomplished. One of the McShane brothers was dead.

The woods were full of gunfire and confusion as the rest of Fargo's group joined in the fight. Fargo glided through the trees. Another of the river pirates suddenly loomed up in front of him. The gun in the man's hand blasted, so close that it practically singed Fargo's eyebrows. He rammed the barrel of the rifle into the pirate's midsection, causing him to double over in pain. Fargo lifted the Henry and brought the butt down on the back of the man's neck. He didn't hold back any this time, and the sharp crack as the blow landed told him that he had just broken the pirate's neck. The man fell and didn't move again.

Another gun roared behind Fargo. He dived forward, twisting as he fell. The hot breath of the slug fanned his bearded cheek. Flame gouted from the Henry's muzzle. The man who had just taken the shot at Fargo was thrown backward by the bullet that slammed into his chest.

Fargo scrambled up and ran toward the skid road. He wanted to find Isabel and the others and make sure they were all right. As he came into the cleared area, he saw Caleb Thorn, Rollie Burnley, and Jasper Milton kneeling behind stumps and firing toward the trees. In the clearing where the walls of the bunkhouse were now on fire, men ran from the burning building and joined the fight, sometimes grappling hand to hand with the pirates. One of the loggers, instead of using a gun, had an ax in each hand and used them to lay into a knot of pirates. The slaughter was a bloody one and ended with the ax-wielder sinking to the ground with several bullets in his chest, but not before he had chopped a half dozen of the pirates into pieces.

Fargo spotted Isabel and saw her use her pistol to gun down one of the attackers. But an instant later, Red Mike McShane lunged up behind her, slammed the barrel of his gun across her wrist, and knocked the pistol out of her hand. Even with all the noise and confusion going on, Fargo heard Isabel cry out in pain as the blow landed. Rage welled up inside him.

Before he could take a shot at McShane, Red Mike had grabbed Isabel and looped an arm around her throat. "Fargo!" he shouted as he twisted around, maintaining his cruel grip on Isabel with one arm and brandishing a revolver in the other hand. "Fargo, where the hell are you?"

"Right here," Fargo called as he stepped out into the open.

Red Mike swung toward him, jerking Isabel with him to use her as a shield. "Fargo," he said as he jutted the gun in his hand at the Trailsman. "How the hell did you get loose?"

"Your girl let us go," Fargo said, giving McShane a slightly simplified answer.

Red Mike stared at him over Isabel's shoulder. "Til-lie?" he exclaimed in disbelief. "Why the hell would she do that?"

"Because she wants you and your brother dead. Because of the way the two of you treated her." With his left hand, Fargo touched his cheek, indicating the terrible scar that Red Mike had inflicted on Tillie.

The leader of the river pirates sneered. "The bitch had it comin'," he said. "She wouldn't do what I told her. She should've known she couldn't get away with that." He raised his voice and shouted, "Linus! I got Fargo! Linus!"

"He can't hear you," Fargo said. "He's lying back there in the trees with his throat shot out."

"You bastard! You lyin' bastard!"

Fargo shook his head. "No. It's the truth, Mike. And this is all over. Your men are beaten. You might as well throw down that gun and give up while you still can. The scheme that you and your sister and Dirkson cooked up will all come out in the open now."

The gun shook in Red Mike's hand. "Go to hell!" he screeched at Fargo.

Captain Andy Russell stepped up behind him and said, "No, *you* go to hell, Mike."

McShane twisted around, taken by surprise, and at that moment Isabel tore free of his grip. She had the sense to fall straight to the ground at his feet, and as soon as she was clear, Fargo and Russell both fired.

Their bullets tore through Red Mike from different but equally deadly angles. He staggered and managed to stay on his feet for a second as blood welled from his mouth. When he tried to lift the gun in his hand toward Isabel, Fargo shot him again, this time through the head. McShane went down hard, dead before he hit the ground.

As Fargo lowered the Henry, he realized that silence had fallen over the woods, broken only by the crackling of flames from the burning bunkhouse. He looked around and saw that Kiley's loggers had gotten the best of the other pirates, killing most of them and capturing the others. Caleb Thorn was talking to one of Kiley's men, pointing out Fargo and explaining the situation.

The logger came over to Fargo and stuck out his hand. "We're much obliged to you, mister," he said. "Those damned pirates would've wiped us out, more'n likely, if you hadn't come along and helped even the odds a little."

Fargo shook hands with him and said, "Sorry we didn't get here in time to keep you from losing your bunkhouse."

"Don't worry about that," the logger said with a grin. "We can build another one. If there's one thing there's plenty of in these parts, it's logs!"

He turned to shout orders to the rest of the crew. They began pitching buckets of water from a nearby slough onto the flames, not in an attempt to save the bunkhouse, since it was too far gone for that, but to keep the blaze from spreading. Forest fires were rare in these piney woods because of all the rain in the area; the trees seldom got dried out enough for a conflagration to spread rapidly. But fire was still a deadly danger in any forest, so the men moved quickly to bring this one under control.

"Are you all right?" Fargo asked Isabel. He had already seen that Russell, Thorn, Burnley, and Milton had come through the battle without any new injuries.

"I'm fine," she told him as she hugged him hard for a brief moment. As she stepped back, she looked up at him and asked, "What are we going to do now, Skye?"

"We're going back to Jefferson," Fargo said as a grim expression appeared on his weary face. "I want to break the news to Francine Baxter that her brothers are dead . . . and her scheme to make her husband the biggest timber baron in these parts and then take over his empire is dead, too."

14

The boss of the logging camp had his men hitch up a team of mules to one of the supply wagons, and Fargo and the rest of the group from the *Bayou Princess* took it back to Jefferson. The hour was late when the wagon rolled into the settlement with Fargo handling the reins. He brought the vehicle to a stop in front of Dr. John Fearn's house.

"You'd better have the doc see to that arm of yours, Cap'n Andy," Fargo told Russell. The frenzied activity of the night had finally caused the wound on Russell's arm to start bleeding again.

"I'd rather go with you and see the showdown with the Baxter woman," Russell complained. "And what about Nick Dirkson?"

"He'll be dealt with in good time," Fargo promised.

"Please, Cap'n Andy," Isabel said from the driver's seat beside Fargo. "You have to take care of yourself so you can see to the repairs on the *Bayou Princess*."

Russell grimaced. "Don't know if that poor riverboat will ever float again, but I guess I owe her a good try." He climbed down from the back of the wagon with Caleb Thorn's help.

"I'll make sure this old pelican behaves himself," Thorn said.

Russell snorted. "Old pelican, is it? You fit the description better than I do, you peg-legged scarecrow."

Fargo grinned as the two old-timers went up the walk toward the doctor's front door.

Burnley and Milton got out of the wagon, too. "If it's all right with you, we're gonna go over to the Snappin' Turtle and have a drink," Milton said.

"Or a dozen," Burnley added.

"Go ahead," Fargo told them. "Sorry the trip down the bayou didn't go like we planned, boys."

"Don't worry about that. Are you sure you'll be all right?"

Fargo nodded. "I'm sure."

Isabel linked her arm with his. "Anyway," she said, "he won't be alone when he confronts that witch."

Fargo shook his head. "You've done enough. I'm dropping you off at the Excelsior House."

"Skye! No!"

He had expected her to argue. "You've risked your life enough tonight," he told her. "You could've been killed half a dozen times over."

"So could you!"

"That's different," Fargo said.

Isabel sniffed. "I don't see why."

Fargo flapped the reins and got the mules moving again. As the wagon rolled toward the hotel, he said, "I've worried about you enough tonight, Isabel. I want a clear head and no distractions when I confront Francine Baxter and her husband."

"So you're saying I'm just a worry to you—is that it?"

Fargo chuckled. He should have known better than to think that he could win an argument with her. "I'll lock you in your room at the hotel if I have to."

"You would, too, you . . . you *man*!"

"Guilty as charged," Fargo said.

Isabel subsided into a sullen silence. Fargo brought the wagon to a halt in front of the Excelsior House, helped her down, and took her up to her room, past the startled eyes of the clerk, who stared at Isabel's mannish attire and the generally mud-stained and disheveled appearance of both of them.

"Do I need to lock the door from outside and take the key with me?" Fargo asked.

"No," she said, breaking her silence. "I'll stay here . . . on one condition."

"What's that?"

"You come back here when you're done and spend the rest of the night making love to me."

Fargo grinned and said, "Deal."

As he left the hotel and looked along the street, he spotted Sheriff Higgins. The lawman's eyes widened in surprise as he saw Fargo striding toward him.

"I thought you'd left town," Higgins said. "Heard rumors you'd gone to Shreveport to fetch some real law." His lips curled in a sneer as he spoke.

"That was the plan," Fargo replied. "Things didn't work out that way, though. Instead, Red Mike McShane's gang of river pirates was broken up when they attacked Kiley's main camp. The McShane brothers are dead, and most of the other members of the gang are, too. The rest have been taken prisoner, and Kiley's men will be bringing them into town in the morning for you to lock up." Fargo had saved his most telling shot for last. "To save their own necks from the hangman's noose, I reckon they'll probably testify that Francine Baxter and Nick Dirkson were behind all the trouble."

Higgins took a deep breath and rocked back on his heels. "Mrs. Baxter?" he said. Fargo's instincts told him that the lawman was genuinely surprised.

"That's right," he said with a nod. "Her maiden name was McShane. She's the sister of Red Mike and Linus. She and Dirkson have been working behind her husband's back all along to wipe out Kiley, but as soon as they had done that, they would have murdered Jonas Baxter and taken over his operation."

"You . . . you can prove all this?" Higgins asked, obviously aghast.

Fargo nodded. "That's right. I'm on my way to the Baxter house now to confront her."

Higgins frowned for a long moment, rubbing his heavy jaw as he thought. Finally he said, "I'll come with you, Fargo. The law needs to be on hand for this. And whether you believe me or not, I'm still the law in this town. And I'm *not* crooked. I reckon Mrs. Baxter and Dirkson had me fooled, too, just like her husband."

It was Fargo's turn to think it over, and after a second, he nodded, too. True, Higgins had picked sides in the conflict between Kiley and Baxter, something an honest lawman never should have done, but Fargo believed now that Higgins hadn't been part of the scheme hatched by Francine and Dirkson.

"Let's go," he said.

They walked side by side to the Baxter house, which was dark at this hour except for a small light in the parlor. Higgins rapped on the door. When it swung open, Francine stood there, dressed in a silk wrapper. Her breath hissed between her teeth as she saw Fargo standing on the porch.

"Surprised to see me?" he asked with a grim smile. "You figured I'd be gator bait before too much longer, didn't you, Mrs. Baxter?"

She recovered quickly, and he had to give her credit for that. "I don't know what you're talking about, Mr. Fargo," she said in a cool voice. "I'm tired of you harassing me and my husband, though. Sheriff, would you be so kind as to escort Mr. Fargo away from here?"

"I'm sorry, Mrs. Baxter, but he's got some mighty interesting things to say," Higgins replied. "Things that need clearin' up. Where's your husband?"

"He's upstairs asleep."

"Why don't you go get him?"

Francine shook her head. "I refuse to disturb him

for something like this. He's a busy man and needs his rest."

"And all you're doing is protecting him, right, Frannie?" Fargo asked with a knowing smile.

Her features twisted again, but before she could reply, she was jerked back out of the way and Nick Dirkson appeared in the doorway, a gun in his hand. He pointed it at Fargo and Higgins and said, "Get in here, you two."

"Nick, no!" Francine said. "You've ruined everything! Now they know—"

"They already knew," Dirkson grated. "You told me yourself that Fargo knows about your brothers, and about what you've been doing with me. And Higgins wouldn't be here if Fargo hadn't told him about it, too."

Higgins said, "Better put down that gun, Dirkson. You're just gonna make things worse for yourself."

"I don't think so," Dirkson replied with an ugly grin. "Now get in here, or I'll shoot you both down right here and now."

"Better do as he says, Sheriff," Fargo advised.

Dirkson backed away from the door, gesturing with the pistol for Fargo and Higgins to follow him. They walked into the foyer, and Francine shut the door behind them. "What are we going to do?" she asked Dirkson, and her voice was practically a moan of despair.

"We'll get rid of these two troublemakers," Dirkson said. "That's what we're gonna do."

"But other people probably know about what's been going on—"

"Who? Kiley? That riverboat captain and the slut Fargo's been spending time with? Who's going to believe them? Not your husband, that's for sure." Dirkson laughed. "Jonas is so stupid he'll believe anything you tell him. He always has, ever since he fell in love with you."

"Is Baxter really upstairs?" Fargo asked. The question was genuine, although he was also stalling for time, waiting for a chance to turn the tables on Dirkson.

"Yeah, he's upstairs," Dirkson said. "Sound asleep, just like Frannie told you. She always slips a little something into the glass of sherry he drinks before bed so he'll sleep right through my visits."

Fargo nodded, not surprised by what Dirkson had just said.

"What about my brothers?" Francine asked. "If you got away from them—"

"The attack on Kiley's camp failed," Fargo said. He didn't sugarcoat the news. "Your brothers are both dead, and so are most of their men. The others were captured, and I reckon they'll tell everything they know in order to save their own hides."

Francine looked at Dirkson. "We've got to run, Nick," she said. "We can't stay here now."

Dirkson's face worked in rage and frustration. "Damn you, Fargo!" he spat. "This was a mighty nice scheme until you came along and ruined it. Baxter never would have figured out what was going on—"

"That's where you're wrong, Nick," a new voice said from the stairway. "I *did* figure it out. That's why I only pretended to drink that glass of sherry tonight."

Everyone's eyes went to the stairs. Jonas Baxter stood there, a stricken look on his rugged face. He had a gun in his hand, too, and it was pointed right at his wife.

"I didn't want to believe it, Francine," Baxter said in a tortured voice. "I didn't want to believe you'd betray me that way. I hoped I was wrong. But I had to know. I'd seen the way you and Dirkson looked at each other when you didn't think I was watching. I knew things were going on that I hadn't ordered. Sure, I wanted to beat Kiley, but not by using those river pirates! And now I find out the McShanes were your brothers—"

Francine took a step toward him. "Jonas, please—"

"The hell with this," Dirkson muttered, and he pulled the trigger.

Fargo saw Dirkson's finger tense on the trigger just before he jerked it. The Trailsman's instincts and reflexes took over. He threw himself sideways, his left shoulder crashing into Higgins and knocking the sheriff off his feet. At the same time Fargo heard the wind-rip of Dirkson's bullet beside his ear. He palmed out his Colt as he fell.

Baxter fired, too, his shot coming hard on the heels of Dirkson's. Francine cried out and staggered back a step.

"No!" Baxter cried. "I didn't mean to—"

The roar of Fargo's gun drowned out the rest of Baxter's words. Dirkson rocked back, the pistol in his hand drooping. As he tried to lift it for a second shot, Fargo squeezed off another round. Like the first, it smashed into Dirkson's chest. Dirkson spun around and folded up, dropping the gun and collapsing on his side. He pawed at his chest as blood ran between his fingers. A final breath rattled in his throat as death claimed him.

Fargo leaped up and swung toward Francine as Baxter dropped his gun and rushed down the stairs. Francine had sunk into a sitting position with her back against the door. The front of her dressing gown was stained with blood, and the stain was growing. She looked up at Baxter and opened her mouth to say something, but before she could get the words out, the life went out of her eyes. They turned glassy as they stared straight ahead.

Baxter fell to his knees in front of her, clutched her lifeless body to him, and began to cry. His back shook as the agonized sobs racked his entire body.

"Holy hell," Higgins muttered as he climbed to his feet. He shook his head at the grim tableau. Then he looked at Fargo and said, "Thanks for knocking me out of the way. I reckon Dirkson really would've killed us both if he could."

Fargo nodded as he slipped his Colt back in its holster. "Yes, he would have." Then he looked at Baxter and thought that Higgins was only half right. Baxter had survived, but for a long time, maybe the rest of his days, he would be spending his time in hell—the hell of what his wife had done, and how her life had ended.

But there was nothing holy about it.

Another half hour had passed by the time Fargo made the weary climb up the stairs of the Excelsior House to his room on the second floor. In that time the undertaker had been summoned to the Baxter mansion, and Fargo had found Lawrence Kiley and told him everything that had happened.

"It wouldn't surprise me if Baxter pulled out and left this part of the country to you," Fargo had said. "He probably won't want to stay around here. Too many reminders of his wife."

Kiley shook his head. "I wanted to beat the son of a bitch . . . but not this way. I wouldn't wish something like that on my worst competitor."

Fargo agreed. Life had plenty of tricks up its sleeve—and they were seldom good ones.

He went to the door of Isabel's room and knocked softly on it. He had made a promise to her earlier in the evening, and he intended to keep it.

Her voice came from the other side of the door. "Skye?"

"That's right."

"It's unlocked."

Fargo twisted the knob and went in. He stopped short when he saw Isabel. She stood beside the bed, nude, but the expression on her face wasn't one of invitation.

It was fear, pure and simple, and the man who stood behind her with an arm around her neck was the cause of it.

He was around thirty and handsome, with sleek dark hair. What Fargo could see of his suit told him that it was expensive.

"Cutler," Fargo said.

The man smirked at him. "That's right, you bastard. The husband of this slut you've been bedding."

Fargo heard a faint sound behind him and felt the cold ring of a gun barrel press against the back of his neck. He said, "I'd be willing to bet this hombre behind me only has one eye."

A gravelly voice said, "You'd be right about that, mister, but I can still see good enough to blow your damn brains out. Don't you forget it, neither."

Fargo stood very still, not wanting the one-eyed man to get trigger-happy. He said, "What happens now?"

"Now you watch while Gibson and I both give this bitch what she needs," Cutler said, "and then we're going to kill you. After that, Isabel will go back to New Orleans with me and be a proper wife to me from now on."

"You really are crazy as a loon, aren't you?" Fargo muttered.

Cutler's handsome face contorted with rage. "She's mine to do with as I want! No one has the right to interfere with that."

"Gideon," Isabel said, her voice having to strain to get past the arm he had pressed across her throat. "Gideon, I'll never belong to you. No matter what you do to me. You might as well kill me, too."

"Oh, no," Cutler purred. "You're not getting off that easy, my dear. You shouldn't have run away from me. You have to be punished for that."

"Gideon . . ." Isabel drew a deep breath. "Go to hell."

And with that, she lowered her head with a jerk and sunk her teeth hard into his arm.

Cutler cried out in pain, and at the same instant, Fargo went down, twisting away from the gun, diving toward the floor. The gun roared as Gibson pulled the trigger. Fargo felt the sting of burning grains of powder as they hit the back of his neck, but the bullet missed.

Fargo swept a leg around, knocking Gibson's legs out from under him. As the one-eyed man fell, Fargo's hand closed around the handle of the Arkansas toothpick and plucked the big knife from its sheath. He rolled and brought the knife up, drove the blade down into Gibson's chest as the man sprawled on the floor. Gibson gasped in pain, arched his back, and kicked his legs, then sagged down again.

Fargo rolled over and came up on one knee as he drew his gun. Isabel and Cutler were wrestling near the window. Cutler got a hand free and slammed a punch into her face. The blow knocked her sprawling back on the bed. Snarling, Cutler reached under his coat and pulled a pistol from a hidden holster.

Fargo fired before Cutler could bring the gun to bear on either him or Isabel. The Colt roared, and Cutler was flung backward by the heavy bullet that smashed into his body. He crashed through the window and fell over the sill onto the balcony outside. A groan came from him, trailing off into nothingness.

A glance toward the bed told Fargo that Isabel was stunned but otherwise all right. He went to the broken window and looked out. Cutler lay on his back. Enough light came from inside the room for Fargo to see that his eyes were open and staring and devoid of life.

Isabel touched his shoulder. "Skye . . ."

Fargo turned, slipping iron into leather. He put his

arms around her nude, shuddering form and drew her close against him. "It's over," he told her in a half whisper. "You won't ever have to go back there."

He would stay until Isabel had recovered some from everything that had happened, he told himself. He would even do what he could to help Captain Russell get the *Bayou Princess* afloat again, if that was possible. If not, he figured Lawrence Kiley might be willing to invest in a new riverboat. Soon enough, a sternwheeler would be steaming up the bayou with Cap'n Andy at the helm and Isabel playing poker in the salon.

And when that day came, Fargo and the Ovaro would be headed west again, leaving these piney woods behind for the mountains and plains that called out to them, back to the big open sky and the wild frontier that was truly their home.

LOOKING FORWARD!
**The following is the opening
section of the next novel in the exciting
Trailsman series from Signet:**

**THE TRAILSMAN #314
NORTH COUNTRY CUTTHROATS**

*Dakota Territory, 1860—a Russian beauty
with a price on her head,
and a storm-ravaged Christmas
trimmed with lead . . .*

Skye Fargo looked up toward the stable's sashed, frosted window for just an instant, but it was long enough to see the silhouette of a bearded face crowned with a heavy fur hat staring in at him.

He glanced away, and by the time he glanced back, the figure was gone. An instant later, the Trailsman, as Fargo was known on the frontier, had reached inside his buckskin mackinaw and filled his hand with his Colt .44.

The Ovaro stallion, for whom he'd just finished

forking a thick bed of fresh straw against the brittle high-plains cold, nickered and swished his tail at the Trailsman's sudden movement . . . and possibly at the sound and smell of a man outside the barn's chinked log walls.

"Easy, boy," Fargo grumbled, patting the horse's neck.

He wheeled, pushed through the stable door, turned down the wick of the barn's single lit lamp, and felt his way through the heavy shadows toward the small side door near the window. His breath was visible in the cold darkness. He drew the door open quickly, waited a count, then, aiming the Colt straight out in front of him, stepped outside. He looked around, swinging the revolver back and forth before him, finger taut against the trigger.

He was alone.

Nothing but horse apples lying in frozen clumps amid the corral's deep, hoof-pocked snow, furred flakes dancing on the wind under a slate gray sky . . . and fresh footprints in the snow beneath the window to the right of the open door.

The prints arced around from the rear of the barn to the window, then retreated the same way—two separate trails made by one set of soft-soled boots or moccasins. Squinting against the brittle slice of the wind blowing snow against his face, Fargo followed the tracks along the side of the barn. At the barn's rear corner, he ducked through the corral slats, stopped, and frowned.

The retreating set of tracks moved out from the rear of the barn to an unused springhouse sheathed in snow and brush about thirty yards away. The trail, slowly filling in with drifting snow, disappeared around the shake-roofed shed's right side.

The snow sifted. The wind moaned around the buildings of the village behind Fargo, catching the springhouse's half-open door with rustling thumps. In the snow-muffled distance, a dog barked.

Fargo adjusted his grip on the .44's walnut handle, his hand turning cold inside his elkskin gloves. His pulse quickened. The tracks could very well lead him into a trap, but he had little choice but to follow and hope his hearing and reactions were keener than those of his stalker. Retiring to the lodge knowing a predator was hunting him would make for a lousy night's rest and merely postpone the trouble.

Tipping his broad-brimmed, high-crowned hat against the wind and shrugging low in his mackinaw—the temperature was falling quickly as the sun dropped, the steely sky turning darker—he moved forward, placing his boots inside the prints of his stalker. The man's feet were two sizes larger than Fargo's.

The Trailsman crossed the space between the springhouse and the barn quickly and, keeping an eye on his flank, followed the tracks along the side of the small building, the tall, dead brush grabbing at his buckskins. He stopped at the back corner. He edged a look around to the back. The tracks continued to the other side.

Fargo cursed, blinked furry snowflakes from his eyelashes, glanced behind him once more, and stole forward, following the large tracks wide of a dead lilac snugging the springhouse's rear wall. He stopped suddenly. The tracks traced a semicircle around the rear wall, disappearing behind the far side.

Ring Around the Rosy, was it?

A soft thump sounded on his left flank. Fargo spun, crouching and cocking the Colt's hammer, then extending the pistol straight out from his shoulder. A lilac branch bounced under the weight of snow fallen from the edge of the roof above, some still sifting on the wind, glistening dully in the wan, fading light.

Fargo turned again, continued following the large-footed tracks along the side of the springhouse, moving slowly, turning complete circles to keep a sharp eye skinned on his backtrail. Stopping at the building's front corner, he wasn't surprised to find the tracks continuing around the front to the other side.

He cursed under his breath, glanced behind him, then took one step around the springhouse's front corner.

A shadow moved in the tail of his right eye.

He froze, heart hammering.

He began to wheel around, bringing up the .44, but he hadn't turned more than six inches before huge arms snaked around him, pinning his own arms to his sides.

A deep, drumming guffaw sounded, hammering the Trailsman's eardrums, as the big arms wrenched the air from his lungs and, pinning his revolver barrel down against his side, lifted him a good two feet off the ground.

"The ole griz done sprung his trap on ya, Fargo!" The big man behind him guffawed again, squeezing the Trailsman against him so hard that Fargo couldn't suck a breath. "Whaddaya think about that?"

"Grizzly, you son of a bitch!" Fargo rasped, trying to peel one of the big man's hands loose with his own free one. "If you don't put me down, I'm gonna drill a bullet through one of your clodhoppers!"

The arm opened.

Fargo dropped straight down and, slipping in the snow, nearly fell as he turned to stare up into the face of the appropriately named Grizzly Olaffson. Actually, if Fargo remembered right, the man's first name was

Oscar. He had been born in Norway, and his name had changed to Grizzly once he'd crossed the Mississippi nearly forty years ago.

He and Fargo had once competed for scouting work among the wagon train captains hauling their emigrant charges from St. Louis to points west and, occasionally, south into Mexico. Fargo and Grizzly had not only fought together in the waterfront saloons of St. Louis and St. Joseph, but, occasionally—when a woman or a dispute over a card game was involved—each other.

Both had the fist and knife scars to prove it.

"Ha-ha!" Grizzly bellowed, the flaps of his wolf-pelt hat dancing untied about his gray-bearded cheeks. His head was the size of a pumpkin, his shoulders were as wide as the axle of a freight wagon, and he had a good four inches on the Trailsman, all six feet eight of his rugged bulk bedecked in an ankle-length bear coat and high-topped moccasins sewn from a wolverine hide. "You oughta be more careful, lettin' a man sneak up on ya like that. I coulda been a Sioux lookin' fer a nice cinnamon scalp like yourn for sweepin' out my lodge!"

"You crazy bastard." Fargo holstered the Colt.

"Merry Christmas to you, too!"

"What the hell are you doin' here, anyway? I thought you'd shacked up in the Rockies with a Ute woman."

"Ah, shit, that was two squaws and a dance hall girl ago! Hell, I live up here now. Drive the stage between Brule City and Devil's Lake year-round. Beats scoutin', trappin, and buffalo huntin', and the pay's enough to keep me in whores and cee-gars."

"You drive the stage for Craw Bascomb?"

"That's right."

"I'm your new shotgun rider."

"I know. Craw told me. He's been grinnin' like a jackass eatin' cactus ever since you sent word back to the fort you'd take the job. He can't believe his luck, gettin' the great Trailsman his ownself to work the line for him."

"It's just for the winter," Fargo said, hunkering down in his coat and glancing at the sky. "I was planning on heading south but got trapped by that first big storm. Figure I might as well work as lay around the fort or the Brule City saloons." He glanced at Grizzly staring down at him, looking for all the world like some fabled man-beast of the northern wild, his furs, heavy brows, and beard limned with the thickening snow. "It's a pretty easy run, isn't it?"

"Pshaw!" said Grizzly. "Ain't nothin' to it, if you can put up with a few chilblains. And bein' on the trail over Christmas, of course. You just get here?"

When Fargo said he had, Grizzly Olaffson laid a big mitten on his shoulder. "Come on over to the lodge. I'll buy you a Christmas toddy and introduce you to ole Craw himself and the passengers headin' out with us tomorrow. We got us a full load, but with those new skis I put on the coach, we'll slide along slickern' snot on a schoolmarm's bell in mid-July!"

"Hold on." Fargo stopped and turned to the big man, slitting an eye. "You got any more practical jokes up your sleeve, keep 'em there. Cold weather makes me jumpy."

Grizzly laughed and clamped his hand once more on Fargo's shoulder, leading him back toward the barn. "I'll mind my P's and Q's just for you, Skye!"

"Yeah," Fargo grumbled, kicking the snow clumps. "Like hell you will."

He retrieved his Henry rifle and saddlebags from the barn, then followed Grizzly across Brule City's main street to a two-story, stone-and-mortar, shake-roofed house sitting under a couple of stark, sprawling cottonwoods. The place was flanked by the Red River of the North. Sheathed in brush, diamond willows, and more towering cottonwoods, the river was little more than a giant gray snake twisting between its shallow banks.

Crows cawed in the snowy silence around the river.

Nearer Fargo and Grizzly Olaffson, a couple of horseback riders passed on the street, wrapped, bundled, and hunched against the cold. Otherwise, the wood or sod huts and the half dozen false-fronted business establishments of Brule City were quiet, hunkering down for another long, cold night, the night before Christmas Eve—well below zero, no doubt, judging by the last several nights, though the snow might keep the mercury from dropping as obscenely as it had been. The frigid air was rife with the smell of burning wood and roasting meat.

Fargo thought of the Arizona sunshine he would have been enjoying with some dusky-skinned, half-dressed senorita had he not let himself get socked into the North Country in late December, and frustration was a coyote's lonely wail inside him.

Grizzly pushed through the lodge's front door, stomping snow from his boots, and Fargo followed him into the large room—a long bar on the left, tables and deep leather chairs and couches to the right, near a snapping fire in the big stone hearth. A buffalo trophy was mounted on the broad chimney over the hearth, the brown eyes reflecting the fire's glow. A spindly Christmas tree—a small piñon pine—stood to one side of the fire, trimmed with about six candles and a couple of popcorn strings.

A plump half-breed girl, dressed in fur-trimmed buckskins, was serving food and drinks to the half dozen people gathered in the sunken dining area near the fire—stage passengers, probably. The room was too dark, lit only by the fire and a couple of candles, for Fargo to make out much more than silhouetted shapes of four men and two women besides the half-breed serving girl.

Opening his bear coat, Grizzly descended the four wooden steps to the sunken room, then climbed three more to the bar. "Craw Bascomb, look who I found skulkin' around outside in the cold—Skye Fargo, his own self! Skye, meet Craw Bascomb. He runs the line when he ain't ice fishin' for bullheads out on the river, or diddlin' the Injun whores over to Mrs. Sondrial's place on Cottonwood Creek!"

Grizzly threw his head back, his guffaws attracting all eyes in the room.

Sheathed Henry repeater in one hand, saddlebags draped over the opposite shoulder, Fargo mounted the steps to the broad bar. Behind the scarred oak planks stood a hard-faced, long-haired gent in a bloodstained apron. A couple of dressed sage hens lay on the bar before the owner of the Red River Stage Company, who tossed down the cleaver and swiped his right hand on his apron before extending it over the bar toward Fargo. A quick, churlish glance toward Grizzly Olaffson spoke volumes about the man's disdain for his giant, overbearing driver.

"Fargo, I'm honored to have ya on the roll."

Fargo removed his glove with his teeth, shook the man's hand, then dropped the glove on the bar. "I'm happy for the work, since I'm trapped up here, anyway. Like I told you in my note, though, I'll be movin' on in May. I have a contract to lead another wagon train west from St. Louis."

Craw Bascomb grunted. He had a big, hard-jawed face, pitted from a bout with smallpox. He was clean-shaven, and his eyes were set wide, his coarse dark brown hair hanging straight down his back. "Too bad. I could use a permanent man since the previous shotgunner—Walleye Tweed—done got hisself shot."

"A holdup?"

"Nah, we haven't had a holdup in over a year, and that was just some restless French boys from up Canada-way. No, old Walleye's wife found out he was diddling Henrietta there." Bascomb canted his head toward the pudgy half-breed girl pouring out a couple of whiskey shots down the bar to his left. "Walleye's wife, Ella, waited till Walleye was having his morning constitutional, then took his own shotgun, walked out to the privy, and shot him while he was sittin' there over the hole, through the privy's back wall. Both barrels. Ella's still walkin' around town with her arm in a sling."

"Ouch."

"You mean Walleye or Ella?"

"I mean Ella," Fargo said, draping his saddlebags atop the bar, then picking up one of the two glasses of whiskey Bascomb had just filled for him and Grizzly. "Walleye probably didn't feel a thing."

Grizzly chuckled as he removed a mitten and picked up his own glass. "You got that right, Skye. Hell, I found Walleye's shredded heart in Ella's rose patch a good thirty feet away!" He threw back the entire shot, then set the glass on the bar, gestured for a refill. "She only did a night in jail as nobody felt Walleye was worth getting the judge up here from Fargo."

When Bascomb solemnly allowed that Grizzly was right, he refilled Grizzly's and Fargo's glasses once more, then corked the bottle. He picked up the bloody meat cleaver, turned to one of the sage hens, and hacked off a leg. "You can have room three upstairs,

Fargo. Free room and board as long as you work for the company. Free whiskey, too, though that doesn't go for Grizzly, as he'd drink me out of a business."

Grizzly cursed and swabbed his glass out with his tongue. Bascomb hacked off another sage hen leg. "You'll be on the road five nights—two goin', one at the end of the line in Devil's Lake, two more comin' back, so pack plenty of warm socks. Only thing different about tomorrow's run is the Army strongbox. I got it under my bed in the back room. We'll load it on the sleigh tomorrow, first thing."

Fargo reached for his saddlebags, stopped, and turned to Bascomb, who'd continued cutting up the hens and tossing the parts in an iron stew pot. "Strongbox?"

"Yeah, we ship payroll coins to the fort up near Devil's Lake—Fort Totten—on occasion. 'Bout fifteen thousand dollars' worth. Shouldn't be any trouble. Owlhoots are generally holed up in the southern settlements this time of the year. There's no one out in the Dakoty countryside after Thanksgiving 'cept the wolves, Norski farmers, and blanket Injuns, and none of them is better armed than you'll be. Nah," Bascomb said, hacking a sage hen breast in two equal halves, "it's a damn easy run."

"If it's such an easy run," Fargo said, pulling his saddlebags off the bar, "why do you need a shotgun rider in the first place?"

Bascomb opened his mouth to speak but stopped when the latch clicked and the timbered front door opened with a squawk, letting in a howling blast of winter wind. The shadows danced as the fire lunged in the stone hearth, and the candles were reduced to sparks.

Fargo followed Bascomb's and Grizzly's gazes to the front of the room. A young woman with glistening, snow-powdered black hair pulled the door closed, frowning and cursing the wind in what Fargo thought was Russian, before turning to the room, the fire dancing in her lustrous, fear-pinched eyes.

No other series packs this much heat!

THE TRAILSMAN

**Available wherever books are sold or at
penguin.com**

NOWHERE, TEXAS
THE SKELETON LODE
DEATH RIDES A CHESNUT MARE
WHISKEY RIVER
TRAIN TO DURANGO
DEVIL'S CANYON
SIX GUNS AND DOUBLE EAGLES
THE BORDER EMPIRE
AUTUMN OF THE GUN
THE KILLING SEASON
THE DAWN OF FURY
DEATH ALONG THE CIMMARON
RIDERS OF JUDGMENT
BULLET CREEK
FOR THE BRAND
GUNS OF THE CANYONLANDS
BY THE HORNS
THE TENDERFOOT TRAIL
RIO LARGO
DEADWOOD GULCH
A WOLF IN THE FOLD
TRAIL TO COTTONWOOD FALLS
BLUFF CITY